T

The Heir

Vita Sackville-West

ET REMOTISSIMA PROPE

Modern Voices

Modern Voices
Published by Hesperus Press Limited
4 Rickett Street, London sw6 1ru
www.hesperuspress.com

The Heir first published 1922
First published by Hesperus Press Limited, 2008

Designed and typeset by Fraser Muggeridge studio
Printed in Jordan by the Jordan National Press

ISBN: 978-1-84391-448-8

Contents

To B.M.

Foreword

I wrote this story in 1922, or it might be 1921. There can be no indiscretion now in revealing that it was inspired by Groombridge Place, astride the borders of Kent and Sussex.

I had always known Groombridge Place and the two old Misses Sant who lived there. After the death of the last Miss Sant, when the property came up for sale, I went there with a rich and florid South American acquaintance of mine, who thought of buying it, and whose attitude towards it shocked me into writing this story. It shocked me also into inventing my Mr Chase, a purely imaginary character, heir to a tradition he had never envisaged, which caught him so unexpectedly into its toils.

I had not read my story for twenty-seven years, when Mr Martin Secker asked me to let him reprint it. Then I reread it, with that obituary feeling one has towards one's youthful work. Can I let it stand, I wondered? Is it too slight? Is it too mawkishly sentimental? Or is it so sincerely felt that it can still stand on its own legs? Sincerity, as I now know, is not enough; it is not the true touchstone, it is the delusion which drives many a writer into believing himself a better writer than he is. Yet I came to the conclusion that it reflected a mood I had felt then and have felt with increasing melancholy ever since, so here, for better or worse, it is.

– *V.S.-W., Sissinghurst, 1949*

The Heir

Miss Chase lay on her immense red silk four-poster that reached as high as the ceiling. Her face was covered over by a sheet, but as she had a high, aristocratic nose, it raised the sheet into a ridge, ending in a point. Her hands could also be distinguished beneath the sheet, folded across her chest like the hands of an effigy; and her feet, tight together like the feet of an effigy, raised the sheet into two further points at the bottom of the bed. She was eighty-four years old, and she had been dead for twenty-four hours.

The room was darkened into a shadowy twilight. Outside, in a pale, golden sunshine, the birds twittered among the young green of the trees. A thread of this sunshine, alive with golden dust-motes, sundered the curtain, and struck out, horizontally, across the boards of the floor. One of the two men who were moving with all possible discretion about the room, paused to draw the curtains more completely together.

'Very annoying, this delay about the coffin,' said Mr Nutley. 'However, I got off the telegrams to the papers in time, I hope, to get the funeral arrangements altered. It would be very awkward if people from London turned up for the funeral on Thursday instead of Friday – very awkward indeed. Of course, the local people wouldn't turn up; they would know the affair had had to be put off; but London people – they're so *scattered*. And they would be annoyed to find they had given up a whole day to a country funeral that wasn't to take place after all.'

'I should think so, indeed,' said Mr Chase, peevishly. 'I know the value of time well enough to appreciate that.'

'Ah yes,' Mr Nutley replied with sympathy, 'you're anxious to be back at Wolverhampton, I know. It's very annoying to have one's work cut into. And if you feel like that about it, when the old lady was your aunt, what would comparative strangers from London feel, if they had to waste a day?'

They both looked resentfully at the stiff figure under the sheet on the bed, but Mr Chase could not help feeling that the solicitor was a little over-inclined to dot his 'i's in the avoidance of any possible hypocrisy. He reflected, however, that it was, in the long run, preferable to the opposite method of Mr Farebrother, Nutley's senior partner, who was at times so evasive as to be positively unintelligible.

Camden!

'Very tidy, everything. H'm – handkerchiefs, gloves, little bags of lavender in every drawer. Yes, just what I should have expected: she was a rare one for having everything spick and span. She'd go for the servants, tapping her stick sharp on the boards, if anything wasn't to her liking; and they all scuttled about as though they'd been wound up after she'd done with them. I don't know what you'll do with the old lady's clothes, Mr Chase. They wouldn't fetch much, you know, with the exception of the lace. There's fine, real lace here, that ought to be worth something. It's all down in the heirloom book, and it'll have to be unpicked off the clothes. But for the rest say twenty pounds. These silk dresses are made of good stuff, I should say,' observed Mr Nutley, fingering a row of black dresses that hung inside a cupboard, and that as he stirred them moved with the faint rustle of dried leaves, 'take my advice, and give some to the housekeeper; that'll be of more value to you in the end than the few pounds you might get for them. Always get the servants on your side, is my axiom. However, it's your affair; you're the sole heir, and there's nobody to interfere.' He said this with a sarcastic inflection detected only by himself; a warning note under the ostensible deference of his words as though daring Chase to assert his rights. 'And, anyway,' he concluded, 'we're not likely to find any more papers in here, so we're wasting time now. Shall we go down?'

'Wait a minute, listen: what's that noise out in the garden?'

'Oh, that! One of the peacocks screeching. There are at least fifty of the damned birds. Your aunt wouldn't have one of them killed, not one. They ruin a garden. Your aunt liked the garden, and she liked the peacocks, but she liked the peacocks better than the garden. Screech, screech – you'll soon do away with them. At least, I should say you would do away with them if you were going to live here. I can see you're a man of sense.'

Mr Chase drew Mr Nutley and his volubility out on to the landing, closing the door behind him. The solicitor ruffled the sheaf of papers he carried in his hand, trying to peep between the sheets that were fastened together by an elastic band.

'Well,' he said briskly, 'if you're agreeable I think we might go downstairs and find Farebrother and Colonel Stanforth. You see, we are trying to save you all the time we possibly can. What about the old lady? Do you want anyone sent in to sit with her?'

'I really don't know,' said Chase, 'what's usually done? You know more about these things than I do.'

'Oh, as to that, I should think I ought to!' Nutley replied with a little self-satisfied smirk. 'Perhaps you won't believe me, but most weeks I'm in a house with a corpse. There are usually relatives, of course, but in this case if you wanted anyone sent in to sit with the old lady, we should have to send a servant. Shall I call Fortune?'

'Perhaps you had better – but I don't know: Fortune is the butler, isn't he? Well, the butler told me all the servants were very busy.'

'Then it might be as well not to disturb them? At any rate, the old lady won't run away,' said Mr Nutley jocosely.

'No, perhaps we needn't disturb them.' Chase was relieved to escape the necessity of giving an order to a servant.

They went downstairs together.

'Hold on to the banisters, Mr Chase; these polished stairs are very tricky. Fine old oak; solid steps too; but I prefer a drugget myself. Good gracious, how that peacock startled me! Look at it, sitting, on the ledge outside the window. It's pecking at the panes with its beak. Shoo, you great gaudy thing.' The solicitor flapped his arms at it, like a skinny crow beating its wings.

They stopped to look at the peacock, which, walking the outside ledge with spread tail, seemed to form part, both in colour and pattern, of the great heraldic window on the landing of the staircase. The sunlight streamed through the colours, and the square of sunlight on the boards was chequered with patches of violet, red and indigo.

'Gaudy?' said Chase. 'It's barbaric. Like jewels. Astonishing.'

Mr Nutley glanced at him with a faint contempt. Chase was a sandy, weakly-looking little man, with thin reddish hair, freckles, and washy blue eyes. He wore an old Norfolk jacket and trousers that did not match; Mr Nutley, in his quick impatient mind, set him aside as reassuringly insignificant.

'Farebrother and Colonel Stanforth are in the library, I believe,' Nutley suggested.

'Don't forget to introduce me to Colonel Stanforth,' said Chase, dismayed at having to meet yet another stranger. 'He was an intimate friend of my aunt's, wasn't he? Is he the only trustee?'

'The other one died and was never replaced. As for Colonel Stanforth being an intimate friend of the old lady, he was indeed; about the only friend she ever had; she frightened everybody else away,' said Nutley, opening the library door.

'Ah, Mr Chase!' Mr Farebrother exclaimed in a relieved and propitiatory tone.

'We've been through all the drawers,' Mr Nutley said, his briskness redoubled in his partner's presence. 'We've got all the necessary papers – they weren't even locked up – so now we can get to business. With any luck Mr Chase ought to see himself back at Wolverhampton within the week, in spite of the delay over the funeral. I've told Mr Chase that it isn't strictly correct to open the papers before the funeral is over, but that, having regard to his affairs in Wolverhampton, and in view of the fact that there are no other relatives whose susceptibilities we might offend, we are setting to work at once.'

He was bending over the table, sorting out the papers as he talked, but now he looked up and saw Chase still standing in embarrassment near the door. 'Dear me, I was forgetting. Mr Chase, you don't know Colonel Stanforth, your trustee, I think? Colonel Stanforth has lived outside the park gates all his life, and I wager he knows every acre of your estate better than you ever will yourself, Mr Chase.'

Mr Farebrother, a round little rosy man in large spectacles, smiled benignly as Chase and Stanforth shook hands. He liked bringing the heir and the trustee together, but his pleasure was clouded by Nutley's last remark, suggesting as it did that Chase would never have the opportunity of learning his estate; he felt this remark to be in poor taste.

'Oh, come! I hope we shall have Mr Chase with us for some time,' he said pleasantly, 'although,' he added, recollecting himself, 'under such melancholy circumstances.' He had never been known to make any more direct allusion to death than that contained in this or similarly consecrated phrases. Mr Nutley pounced instantly upon the evasion.

'After all, Farebrother, Chase never knew the old lady, remember. The melancholy part of it, to my mind, is the muddle the estate is in. Mortgaged up to the last shilling, and overrun with peacocks. Won't you come and sit at the table, Mr Chase? Here's a pencil in case you want to make any notes.'

Colonel Stanforth came up to the table at the same time. Chase shied away, and went to sit on the window-seat. Mr Farebrother began a little preamble.

'We sent for you immediately, Mr Chase; that is to say, Colonel Stanforth, who was on the spot at the moment of the regrettable event, communicated with us and with you simultaneously. We should like to welcome you, with all the sobriety required by the cloud which must hang over this occasion, to the estate which has been in the possession of your family for the past five hundred years. We should like to express our infinite regret at the embarrassments under which the estate will be found to labour. We should like to assure you – I am speaking now for my partner and myself – that our firm has been in no way responsible for the management of the property. Miss Chase, your aunt, whom I immensely revered, was a lady of determined character and charitable impulses...'

'You mean, she was an obstinate old sentimentalist,' said Mr Nutley, losing his patience.

Mr Farebrother looked gently pained.

'Charitable impulses,' he repeated, 'which she was always loath to modify. Colonel Stanforth will tell you that he has had many a discussion...' ('I should just think so,' said Colonel Stanforth, 'you could argue the hind leg off a donkey, but you couldn't budge Phillida Chase,') 'there were questions of undesirable tenants and what not – I confess it saddens me to think of Blackboys so much encumbered...'

'Encumbered! My good man, the place will be in the market as soon as I can get it there,' said Mr Nutley, interrupting again, and tapping his pencil on the table.

'It would have been so pleasant,' said Mr Farebrother sighing, 'if matters had been in an entirely satisfactory condition, and our duty towards Mr Chase would have been so joyfully fulfilled. Your family, Mr Chase, were Lords of the Manor of Blackboys long before any house was built upon this site. The snapping of such a chain of tradition...'

'Out of date, out of date, my good man,' said Nutley, full of contempt and surprisingly spiteful.

'Let's get on to the will,' suggested Stanforth.

Mr Nutley produced it with alacrity.

'Dear, dear,' said Mr Farebrother, wiping his spectacles. The reading of a will was to him always a painful proceeding. It was indeed an unkind fate which had cast one of his amiable and conciliatory nature into the melancholy regions of the law.

'It's very short,' said Nutley, and read it aloud.

After providing for a legacy of five hundred pounds to the butler, John Fortune, in recognition of his long and devoted service, and for a legacy of two hundred and fifty pounds to her friend Edward Stanforth 'in anticipation of services to be rendered after my death,' the testator devised the Manor of Blackboys and the whole of the Blackboys Estate and all other messuages tenements hereditaments and premises situate in the counties of Kent and Sussex and elsewhere and all other estates and effects whatsoever and wheresoever both real and personal to her nephew Peregrine Chase at present of Wolverhampton.

'Sensible woman – she got a solicitor to draw up her will,' said Mr Nutley as he ended, 'no sidetracks, no ambiguities, no bother. Sensible woman. Now we can get to work.'

'Ah, dear!' said Mr Farebrother in wistful reminiscence, 'how well I remember the day Miss Chase sent for me to assist her in the making of that will; it was just such a day as this, and after I had been waiting a little while she came into the room, a black lace scarf on her white hair, and her beautiful hands leaning on the top of her stick – she had very beautiful hands, your aunt, Mr Chase, beautiful cool ivory hands – and I remember she was singularly gracious, singularly gracious; a great lady of the old school, and she was pleased to twit me about my reluctance to admit that some day even *she*... ah, well, will-making is a painful matter; but I remember her, gallant as ever...'

'That's all rubbish, Farebrother,' said Mr Nutley rudely, as his partner showed signs of meandering indefinitely on, 'gracious, indeed! When you know she terrified you nearly out of your life. You always get mawkish like this about people once they're dead.'

Mr Farebrother blinked mildly, and Nutley continued without taking any further notice of him.

'You haven't done so well out of this as John Fortune,' he said to Stanforth, 'and you'll have a deal more trouble.'

'I take it,' said Stanforth, getting up and striding about the room, 'that in the matter of this estate there are a great many liabilities and no assets to speak of, except the estate itself? To start with, there's a twenty-thousand-pound mortgage. What's the income from the farms?'

'A bare two thousand a year.'

'So you start the year with a deficit, having paid off your income tax and the interest on the mortgage. Disgusting,' said Stanforth. 'One thing, at any rate, is clear: the place must go. One could just manage to keep the house, of course, but I don't see how anyone could afford to live in it, having kept it. The land isn't worth over much, but luckily we've got the house and gardens. What figure, Nutley? Thirty thousand? Forty?'

Mr Nutley whistled.

'You're optimistic. The house isn't so very large, and it's inconvenient, no bathrooms, no electric light, no garage, no central heating. The buyer would have all that on his hands, and the moat ought to be cleaned out too. It's insanitary.'

'Still, the house is historical,' said Stanforth, 'I think we can safely say thirty thousand for the house. It's a perfect specimen of Elizabethan, so I've always been told, and has the Tudor moat and outbuildings into the bargain. Thirty thousand for the house,' he noted on a piece of paper.

'I wouldn't care for it myself,' said Mr Nutley, looking round, 'low rooms, dark passages, a stinking moat, and a slippery staircase. If that's Tudor, you're welcome to it.' His voice had a peculiarly malignant intonation. 'Still, it's a gentleman's place, I don't deny, and ought to make an interesting item under the hammer.' He passed the tip of his tongue over his lips, a gesture horridly voluptuous in one so sharp and meagre.

'Then we have the furniture and the tapestries and the pictures,' Stanforth went on. 'I think we might reckon another twenty thousand for them. Americans, you know – or the buyer of the house might care for some of the furniture. The pictures aren't of much value, so I understand, save as of family interest. Twenty thousand. That clears off the mortgage. What about the farms and the land?'

'You could split some of the park up into building lots,' said Mr Nutley.

Mr Farebrother gave a little exclamation.

'The park – it's a pretty park, Nutley.'

'Very pretty, and any builder who chose to run up half a dozen villas would be a sensible chap,' Mr Nutley replied, wilfully misunderstanding him. 'I should suggest a site at the top of the hill, where you get the view. What do you think, Colonel Stanforth?'

'I think the buyer of the house should be given the option of buying in the whole of the park, that section being reserved at the price of accommodation land, if he chooses to pay for it.'

Mr Nutley nodded. He approved of Colonel Stanforth as an adequately shrewd business man.

'There remain the farm lands,' he said, referring to his papers. 'Two thousand acres, roughly; three good farm houses; and a score of cottages. It's a little difficult to price. Say, taking one thing in with another, twenty pounds an acre, including the buildings – a good deal of the land is worthless. Forty thousand. We've disposed now of all the assets. We shall be lucky if we can clear the death duties and mortgage out of the proceeds of the sale, and let Mr Chase go with whatever amount the house itself fetches to bring him in a few hundreds a year for the rest of his life.'

They stared across at Chase, whose concern with the affair they appeared hitherto to have forgotten. Mr Farebrother alone kept his eyes bent down, as very meticulously he sharpened the point of his pencil.

'It's an unsatisfactory situation,' said Mr Nutley, 'if I were Chase I should resent being dragged away from my ordinary business on such an unprofitable affair. He'll be lucky, as you say, if he clears the actual value of the house for himself after everything is settled up. Now, are we to try for auction or private treaty? Personally I think the house at any rate will go by private treaty. The present tenants will probably buy in their own farms. But the house, if it's reasonably well advertised, ought to attract a number of private buyers. We must have a decent caretaker to show people over the place. I suggest the present butler? He was in Miss Chase's service for thirty years.' He looked around for approval; Chase and Stanforth both nodded, though Chase felt so much of an outsider that he wondered whether Nutley would consider him justified in nodding. 'Ring the bell, Farebrother, will you? It's just behind you. Look at the bell, gentlemen! What an antiquated arrangement! There's no doubt, the house is terribly inconvenient.'

Fortune, the butler, came in, a thin grizzled man in decent black.

'Perhaps you had better give your instructions, Nutley,' Chase said from the window-seat as the solicitor glanced at him with conventional hesitation.

'I'm speaking for Mr Chase, Fortune,' said Mr Nutley. 'Your late mistress' will unfortunately isn't very satisfactory, and Blackboys will be in the market before very long. We want you to stay on until then, with such help as you need, and you must tell the other servants they have all a month's notice. By the way, you inherit five hundred pounds under the will, but it'll be some time before you get it.'

'Blackboys in the market?' Fortune began.

'Oh, my good man, don't start lamenting again here,' exclaimed Mr Nutley hurriedly, 'think of those five hundred pounds – a very nice little sum of which we should all be glad, I'm sure.'

'Dear me, dear me,' said Mr Farebrother, much distressed, and he got up and patted Fortune on the shoulder.

Nutley was collecting the papers again into a neat packet, boxing them together on the table as though they had been a pack of cards. He glanced up to say,

'That settled, Fortune? Then we needn't keep you any longer; thanks. Well, Mr Chase, if there's anything we can do for you tomorrow, you have only to ring me up or Farebrother – oh, I forgot, of course, you aren't on the telephone here.'

Chase, who had been thinking to himself that Nutley was a splendid man – really efficient, a first-class man, was suddenly aware that he resented the implied criticism.

'I can go to the post office if I want to telephone,' he said coldly.

Mr Farebrother noticed the coldness in his tone, and thought regretfully, 'Dear me, Nutley has offended him – ignored him completely all the time. I ought to have put that right – very remiss of me.'

He said aloud, 'If Mr Chase would prefer not to sleep in the house, I should be very glad to offer him hospitality…'

'Afraid of the old lady's ghost, Chase?' said Mr Nutley with a laugh that concealed a sneer.

They all laughed, with exception of Mr Farebrother, who was pained.

Chase was tired; he wished they would go; he wanted to be alone.

2

He was alone; they had gone, Stanforth striding off across the park in his rather ostentatious suit of large checks and baggy knickerbockers, the two solicitors, with their black leather handbags, trundling down the avenue in the station cab. They had gone, they and their talk of mortgages, rents, acreage, tenants, possible buyers, building lots, and sales by auction or private treaty! Chase stood on the bridge above the moat, watching their departure. He was still a little confused in his mind, not having had time to turn round and think since Stanforth's telegram had summoned him that morning. Arrived at Blackboys, he had been immediately commandeered by Nutley, had had wishes and opinions put into his mouth, and had found a complete set of intentions ready-made for him to assume as his own. That had all saved him a lot of trouble, undoubtedly; but nevertheless he was glad of a breathing space; there were things he wanted to think over; ideas he wanted to get used to...

He was poor; and hardworking in a cheerless fashion; he managed a branch of a small insurance company in Wolverhampton, and expected nothing further of life. Not very robust, his days in an office left him with little energy after he had conscientiously carried out his business. He lived in lodgings in Wolverhampton, smoking rather too much and eating rather too little. He had neither loved nor married. He had always known that some day, when his surviving aunt was dead, he would inherit Blackboys, but Blackboys was only a name to him, and he had gauged that the inheritance would mean for him little but trouble and interruption, and that once the whole affair was wound up he would resume his habitual existence just where he had dropped it.

His occupations and outlook might thus be comprehensively summarised.

He turned to look back at the house. Any man brighter-hearted and more optimistic might have rejoiced in this enforced expedition as a holiday, but Chase was neither optimistic nor bright-hearted. He took life with a dreary and rather petulant seriousness, and, full of resentment against this whole unprofitable errand, was dwelling now upon the probable, the almost certain, inefficiencies of his subordinates in Wolverhampton, because he had in him an old-maidish trait that could not endure the thought of other people interfering with his business or his possessions. He worried, in his small anaemic mind that was too restricted to be contemptuous, and too diffident to be really bad tempered... The house looked down at him, grave and mellow. Its façade of old, plum-coloured bricks, the inverted V of the two gables, the rectangles of the windows, and the creamy stucco of the little colonnade that joined the two projecting wings, all reflected unbroken in the green stillness of the moat. It was not a large house; it consisted only of the two wings and the central block, but it was complete and perfect; so perfect, that Chase, who knew and cared nothing about architecture, and whose mind was really absent, worrying, in Wolverhampton, was gradually softened into a comfortable satisfaction. The house was indeed small, sweet, and satisfying. There was no fault to be found with the house. It was lovely in colour and design. It carried off, in its perfect proportions, the grandeur of its manner with an easy dignity. It was quiet, the evening was quiet, the country was quiet; it was part of the evening and the country. The country was almost unknown to Chase, whose life had been spent in towns – factory towns. Here he was on the borders of Kent and Sussex where the nearest town was a village, a jumble of cottages round a green, at his own park gates. The house seemed to lie at the very heart of peace.

A little wooden gate, moss-grown and slightly dilapidated, cut off the bridge from the gravelled entrance space; he shut and latched it, and stood on the island that the moat surrounded. Swallows were swooping along the water, for the air was full of insects in the golden haze of the May evening. Faint clouds of haze hung about, blue and gold, deepening the mystery of the park, shrouding the recesses of the garden. The place was veiled. Chase put out his hand as though to push aside a veil...

He detected himself in the gesture, and glanced round guiltily to see whether he was observed. But he was alone; even the curtains behind the windows were drawn. He felt a desire to explore the garden, but hesitated, timorous and apologetic. Hitherto in his life he had explored only other people's gardens on the rare days when they were opened to the public; he remembered with what pained incredulity he had watched the public helping itself to the flowers out of the borders, for he could not help being a great respecter of property. He prided himself, of course, on being a socialist; that was the fashion amongst the young men he occasionally frequented in Wolverhampton; but unlike them he was a socialist whose sense of veneration was deeper and more instinctive than his socialism. He had thought at the time that he would be very indignant if he were the owner of the garden. Now that he actually was the owner, he hesitated before entering the garden, with a sense of intrusion. Had he caught sight of a servant he would certainly have turned and strolled off in the opposite direction.

The house lay in the hollow at the bottom of a ridge of wooded hills that sheltered it from the north, but the garden was upon the slope of the hill, in design quite simple: a central walk divided the square garden into halves, eased into very flat, shallow steps, and outlined by a low stone coping. A wall surrounded the whole garden. To reach the garden from the house, you crossed a little footbridge over the moat, at the bottom of the central walk. This simplicity, so obvious, yet, like the house, so satisfying, could not possibly have been otherwise ordered; it was married to the lie of the land. It flattered Chase with the delectable suggestion that he, a simple fellow, could have conceived and carried out the scheme as well as had the architect.

He was bound to admit that a simple fellow would not have thought of the peacocks. They were the royal touch that redeemed the gentle friendliness of the house and garden from all danger of complacency. He paused in amazement now at his first real sight of them. All the way up the low wall on either side of the central walk they sat, thirty or forty of them, their long tails sweeping down almost to the ground, the delicate crowns upon their heads erect in a feathery line of perspective, and the blue of their breasts rich above the grey stone coping. Halfway up the walk, the coping was broken by two big stone balls, and upon one of these a peacock stood with his tail fully spread behind him, and uttered his discordant cry as though in the triumph and pride of his beauty.

Chase paused. He was too shy even to disturb those regal birds. He imagined the swirl of colour and the screech of indignation that would accompany his advance, and before their arrogance his timidity was abashed. But he stood there for a very long while, looking at them, until the garden became swathed in the shrouds of the blue evening, very dusky and venerable. He did not pass over the moat, but stood on the little bridge, between the house and the garden, while those shrouds of evening settled with the hush of vespers round him, and as he looked he kept saying to himself, 'Mine? *Mine?*' in a puzzled and deprecatory way.

3

When Fortune showed him his room before dinner he was silent and inclined to scoff. He had been shown the other rooms by Nutley when he first arrived, and had gazed at them, accepting them without surprise, much as he would have gazed at rooms in some showplace or princely palace that he had paid a shilling to visit. The hall, the dining room, the library, the long gallery – he had looked at them all, and had nodded in reply to the solicitor's comments, but not for a moment had it entered his head to regard the rooms as his own. To be left, however, in this room that resembled all the others, and to be told that it was his bedroom; to realise that he was to sleep inside that brocaded four-poster with the ostrich plumes nodding on the top; to envisage the trivial and vulgar functions of his daily dressing and undressing as taking place within this room that although so small was yet so stately – this was a shock that made him draw in his breath. Left alone, his hand raised to give a tug at his tie, he stared round and emitted a soft whistle. The walls were hung with tapestry, a grey-green landscape of tapestry, the borders formed by two fat twisted columns, looped across with garlands of flowers and fruits, and cherubs with distended cheeks blew zephyrs across this woven Arcady. High-backed Stuart chairs of black and gold... Chase wanted to take off his boots, but did not venture to sit down on the tawny cane-work. He moved about gingerly, afraid of spoiling something. Then he remembered that everything was his to spoil if he so chose. Everything waited on his good pleasure; the whole house, all those rooms, the garden; all those unknown farms and acres that Nutley and Stanforth had discussed. The thought produced no exhilaration in him, but, rather, an extreme embarrassment and alarm. He was more than ever dismayed to think that someone, sooner or later, was certain to come to him for orders...

He hesitated for an appreciable time before making up his mind to go down to dinner; in fact, even after he had resolutely pushed open his bedroom door, he still wavered upon its threshold. The landing, lit by the yellow flame of a solitary candle stuck into a silver sconce, was full of shadows: the well of the staircase gaped black; and across the great window red velvet curtains had been drawn, and now hung from floor to ceiling. Down the passage, behind one of those mysterious closed doors, lay the old woman dead in her pompous bed. So the house must have drowsed, evening after evening, before Chase ever came near it, with the only difference that from one of those doors had emerged an old lady dressed in black silk, leaning on a stick, an arbitrary old lady, who had slowly descended the polished stairs, carefully placing the rubber ferrule of her stick from step to step, and helping herself on the banisters with the other hand, instead of the alien clerk from Wolverhampton, who hesitated to go downstairs to dinner because he feared there would be a servant in the room to wait upon him.

There was. Chase dined miserably, and was relieved only when he was left alone, port and madeira set before him, and the four candles reflected in the shining oak table. A greyhound which had joined him at the foot of the stairs, now sat gravely beside him, and he gave him bits of biscuit as he had not dared to do in the presence of the servant. More at his ease at last, he sat thinking what he would do with the few hundreds a year Nutley predicted for him. Not such an unprofitable business after all, perhaps! He would be able to move from his lodgings in Wolverhampton; perhaps he could take a small villa with a little bit of garden in front. His imagination did not extend beyond Wolverhampton. Perhaps he could keep back one or two pieces of plate from the sale; he would like to have something to remind him of his connection with Blackboys and with his family. He cautiously picked up a porringer that was the only ornament on the table, and examined it. It gave him a little shock of familiarity to see that the coat of arms engraved on it was the same as the coat on his own signet ring, inherited from his father, and the motto was the same too: *Intabescantque relictâ*, and the tiny peregrine falcon as the crest. Absurd to be surprised! He ought to remember that he wasn't a stranger here; he was Chase, no less than the old lady had been Chase, no less than all the portraits upstairs were Chase. He had already seen that coat of arms today, in the heraldic window, but without taking in its meaning. It gave him a new sense of confidence now, reassuring him that he wasn't the interloper he felt himself to be.

It was pleasant enough to linger here, with silence and shadows all round the pool of candlelight, that lit the polish of the table, the curves of the silver, and the dark wine in the round-bellied decanters; pleasant to dream of that villa which might now be attainable; but he had better go, or the servant would be coming to clear away.

Rising, he went out into the hall, followed by the dog, who seemed to have adopted him unquestioningly. As Chase didn't know his name, he bent down to read the inscription on the collar, but found only the address: CHASE, BLACKBOYS. That had been the old lady's address, of course, but it would do for him too; he needn't have the collar altered. CHASE, BLACKBOYS. It was simply handed on; no change. It gave him a queer sensation; this coming to Blackboys was certainly a queer experience, interrupting his life. He scarcely knew where he was as yet, or what he was doing; he had to keep reminding himself with an effort.

In the hall he hesitated, uncertain as to which was the door of the library, afraid that if he opened the wrong door he would find himself in the servants' quarters, perhaps even open it on them as they sat at supper. The dog stood in front of one door, wagging his tail and looking up at Chase, so he tried the handle; it was the wrong door, but instead of leading to the servants' quarters it opened straight on to the moonlit garden. The greyhound bounded out and ran about in the moonlight, a wraith of a dog in the ghostly garden. Ghostly... Chase wandered out, up the walk to the top of the hill, where he turned to look down upon the house, folded black in the hollow, the moonlight gleaming along the moat and winking on a window. Not a breath ruffled that milky stillness; the great cloths of light lay spread out over the grass, the blocks of shadow were profound; above the low-lying park trailed a faint white mist, and in a vaporous sky the moon rode calm and sovereign. Chase felt that on a scene so perfectly set something ought to happen. A pity that it should all be wasted... How many such nights must have been wasted! The prodigal loveliness of summer nights, lying illusory under the moon, shamelessly soliciting romance! But nothing happened; there was nothing but Chase looking down on the silent house, looking for a long time down on the silent house, and thinking that, on that night so set for a lovers' meeting, no lovers had met.

4

He was very glad when the funeral was over, and he was rid of all the strange neighbours who had wrung his hand and uttered commiserating phrases. He was also glad that the house should be relieved of the presence of his aunt, for he could tread henceforth unrestrained by the idea that the corpse might rise up and with a pointing finger denounce his few and timorous orders. He stood now on the threshold of the library downstairs, looking at a bowl of coral-coloured tulips whose transparent delicacy detached itself brightly in the sober panelled room. He was grateful to the quietness that slumbered always over the house, abolishing fret as by a calm rebuke.

His recollections of the funeral were, he found to his dismay, principally absurd. Mr Farebrother had sidled up to him, when he thought Nutley was preoccupied elsewhere, as they returned on foot up the avenue after the ceremony. 'A great pity the place should have to go,' Mr Farebrother had said, trotting along beside him, 'such a very great pity.' Chase had agreed in a perfunctory way. 'Perhaps it won't come to that,' said Mr Farebrother with a vague hopefulness. Chase again murmured something in the nature of agreement. 'I like to think things will come right until the moment they actually go wrong,' Mr Farebrother said with a smile. 'Very sad, too, the death of your aunt,' he added. 'Yes,' said Chase. 'Well, well, perhaps it isn't so bad as we think,' said Mr Farebrother, causing Chase to stare at him, thoroughly startled this time by the extent of the rosy old man's optimism.

But he was not now dwelling upon the funeral. Tomorrow he must leave Blackboys. No doubt he would find his affairs in Wolverhampton in a terrible way. He said to himself, 'Tut tut,' his mind absent, though his eyes were still upon the tulips; but his annoyance over the office in Wolverhampton was largely superficial. Business had a claim on him, certainly; the business of his employers; but his own private business had a claim too, that, moreover, would take up but a month or two out of his life; after that Blackboys would be sold, and would engage no more of his time away from Wolverhampton. Blackboys would pass to other hands, making no further demands upon Peregrine Chase. It would be a queer little incident to look back upon; his few acquaintances in Wolverhampton, with whom he sometimes played billiards of an evening, or joined in a whist drive, would stare, derisive and incredulous, if the story ever leaked out, at the idea of Chase as a landed proprietor. As a squire! As the descendant of twenty generations! Why, no one in Wolverhampton knew so much as his Christian name; he had been careful always to sign his letters with a discreet initial, so that if they thought of it at all they probably thought him Percy. A friend would have nosed it out. There was a safeguard in friendlessness. Chase was a reticent little man, as his solicitors had had occasion to remark. Nutley found this very convenient: Chase, making no comment, left him free to manage everything according to his own ideas. Indeed, Nutley frequently forgot his very existence. It was most convenient.

As for Chase, he wondered sometimes absently which he disliked least: Farebrother with his weak sentimentality, or Nutley, who was so astute, so bent upon getting Blackboys brilliantly into the market, and whose grudging respect for old Miss Chase, beneath his impatience of the tyranny she had imposed upon him, was so readily divined.

Chase stood looking at the bowl of tulips; it seemed to him that he spent his days for ever looking at something, and deriving from it that new, quiet satisfaction. He was revolving in his mind a phrase of Mr Farebrother's, to the effect that he ought to go the rounds and call upon his tenants. 'They'll expect it, you know,' Farebrother had said, examining Chase over the top of his spectacles. Chase had gone through a moment of panic, until he remembered that his departure on the morrow would postpone this ordeal. But it remained uncomfortably with him. He had seen his tenants at the funeral, and had eyed them surreptitiously when he thought they were not noticing him. They were all farmers, big, heavy, kindly men, whose manner had adopted little Chase into the shelter of an interested benevolence. He had liked them; distinctly he had liked them. But to call upon them in their homes, to intrude upon their privacy – he who of all men had a wilting horror of intrusion, that was another matter.

He enjoyed being alone himself; he had a real taste for solitude, and luxuriated now in his days and particularly his evenings at Blackboys, when he sat over the fire, stirring the great heap of soft grey ashes with the poker, the ashes that were never cleared away; he liked the woolly thud when the poker dropped among them. Those evenings were pleasant to him; pleasant and new, though sometimes he felt that in spite of their novelty they had been always a part of his life. Moreover he had a companion, for Thane, the greyhound, slim and fawn-coloured, lay by the fire asleep, with his nose along his paws.

There existed in his mind a curious confusion in regard to his tenants, a confusion quite childish, but which carried with it a sort of terror. It dated from the day when, for want of something better to do, he had turned over some legal papers left behind by Nutley, and the dignity of his manor had disclosed itself to him in all the brocaded stiffness of its ancient ritual and phraseology. He had laughed; he could not help laughing; but he had been impressed and even a little awed. The weight of legend seemed to lie suddenly heavy upon his shoulders, and he had gazed at his own hands, as though he expected to see them mysteriously loaded with rough hierarchical rings. Vested in him, all this antiquity and surviving ceremonial! He read again the almost incomprehensible words that had first caught his eye, scraps here and there as he turned the pages. 'There are three teams in demesne, thirty-one villains, with fourteen bordars, i.e., the class who should not pay live heriot. The furrow-long measures forty roods, i.e., forty lengths of the Ox-goad of one hundred and sixty-six feet, a rod just long enough to lie along the yokes of the first three pair of Oxen, and let the ploughman thrust with the point at either flank of either the sod ox or the sward ox. Such a strip four rods in width gives an acre.' 'There is wood of seventy-five Hogs. The Hogs must be panage Hogs, one in seven, paid each year for the right to feed the herd in the Lord of the Manor's wooded wastes.'

What on earth were panage hogs, to which apparently he was entitled?

He read again, 'The quantum of liberty of person and alien-ation originally enjoyed by those now represented by the Free Tenants of the Manor is a matter for argument for the theorists. The free tenants were *liberi homines* within the statute *Quia Emptores Terrarum*, and as such from 1289 could sell their holdings to whomsoever they would, without the Lord's licence, still less without surrender or admittance, saving always the condition that the feoffee do hold of the same Lord as feoffor. And the feoffee must hold, i.e., must acknowledge that he hold. There must be tenure in fact and the Lord must know his new tenant as such. Some privity must be established. The new tenant must do fealty and say "I hold of you, the Lord." An alienation without such acknowledgement is not good against the Lord.'

He laid down the papers. Could such things be actualities? This must be the copy of some old record he had got hold of. But no; he turned back to the first page and found the date of the previous year. It appalled him to think that since such things had happened to his aunt, they were also liable to happen to him. What would he do with a panage hog, supposing one were driven up to the front door? Still less would he know what to do if one of those farmers he had seen at the funeral were to say to him, 'I hold of you, the Lord.'

Then he remembered that he had not found the people in the village alarming. He remembered a conversation he had had the day before, with a man and his wife, as he leaned over the gate that led into their little garden. On either side of the tiled path running up to the cottage door were broad beds filled with a jumble of flowers – pansies, lupins, tulips, honesty, sweet rocket, and bright fragile poppies.

'Lovely show of flowers you have there,' he had said tentatively to a woman in an apron, who stood inside the gate, knitting.

'It's like that all the summer,' she replied, 'my husband's very proud of his garden, he is. But we're under notice to quit.' She spoke with an unfamiliar broad accent and a burr that had prompted Chase to say:

'You're not from these parts?'

'No, sir, I'm from Sussex. It's not a wonderful great matter of distance. I'm wanting my man to come back with me, and settle near my old home, but he says he was born in Kent and in Kent he'll die.'

'That's right,' approved the man who had come up. 'I don't hold with folk leaving their own county. It's like sheep – take sheep away from their own parts, and they don't do near so well. Oxfordshire don't do on Romney Marsh, and Romney Marsh don't do in Oxfordshire.' He was ramming tobacco into his pipe, but broke off to pull a seedling of groundsel out from among his pinks. He crushed it together and put it carefully into his pocket. 'I made this garden,' he resumed, 'carried the mould home on my back evening after evening, and sent the kids out with bodges for road scrapings, till you couldn't beat my soil, sir, not in this village, nor my flowers either. But I'm under notice, and sooner than let them pass to a stranger I'll put my baggin-hook through the roots of every plant amongst them,' he said, and spat.

'Twenty-five years we've lived in this cottage, and brought up ten children,' said the woman.

'The cottage is to come down, and make room for a building site, so Mr Nutley told us,' the man continued.

'We'd papered and whitewashed it ourselves,' said the woman.

'I laid them tiles, sir, me and my eldest boy,' said the man, pointing with the stem of his pipe down at the path, 'rare job it was. There wasn't no garden, not when I came here.'

'Twenty-five years ago,' said the woman.

They both stared mournfully at Chase.

'I'm under notice to quit, too, you know,' said Chase, rather embarrassed, as though they had brought a gentle reproof against him, trying to excuse himself by this joke.

'I know that, sir; we're sorry,' the man had said instantly.

(Sorry. They had never seen him before, yet they were sorry.)

'Miss Chase, your aunt, sir, liked my garden properly,' said the man. 'She'd stop here always, in her pony-chaise, and have a look at my flowers. She'd say to me, chaffing-like, "You've a better show than me, Jakes." But she didn't like peonies. I had a fine clump of peonies and she made me dig it up. Lord, she was a tartar – saving your presence, sir. But a good heart, so nobody took no notice. But peonies – no, she wouldn't have peonies at any price.'

'There's few folks in this village ever thought to see Blackboys in other hands than Chase's,' said the woman. ''Tis the peacocks will be grieved – dear! dear!'

'The peacocks?' Chase had repeated.

'Folks about here do say, the peacocks'll die off when Blackboys goes from Chase's hands,' said the man. 'They be terrible hard on a garden, though, do be peacocks,' he had said further, meticulously removing another weed from among his pinks.

5

That had been an experience to Chase, a milestone on his road. He was to experience much the same sensation when his lands received him. It was a new world to him – new because it was so old – ancient and sober according to the laws of nature. There was here a rhythm which no flurry could disturb. The seasons ordained, and men lived close up against the rulings so prescribed, close up against the austere laws, at once the masters and the subjects of the land that served them and that they as loyally served. Chase perceived his mistake; he perceived it with surprise and a certain reverence. Because the laws were unalterable they were not necessarily stagnant. They were of a solemn order, not arbitrarily framed or admitting of variation according to the caprice of mankind. In the place of stagnation, he recognised stability. And as his vision widened he saw that the house fused very graciously with the trees, the meadows, and the hills, grown there in place no less than they, a part of the secular tradition. He reconsidered even the pictures; not as the representation of meaningless ghosts, but as men and women whose blood had gone to the making of that now in his own veins. It was the land, the farms, the rickyards, the sown, the fallow, that taught him this wisdom. He learnt it slowly, and without knowing that he learnt. He absorbed it in the company of men such as he had never previously known, and who treated him as he had never before been treated – not with deference only, which would have confused him, but with a paternal kindliness, a quiet familiarity, an acquaintance immediately linked by virtue of tradition. To them, he, the clerk of Wolverhampton, was, quite simply, Chase of Blackboys. He came to value the smile in their eyes, when they looked at him, as a caress.

6

When Nutley came again, a fortnight after the funeral, to his surprise he met Chase in the park with Thane, the greyhound, at his heels.

'Good gracious,' he said, 'I thought you were in Wolverhampton?'

'So I was. I thought I'd come back to see how things were going on. I arrived two days ago.'

'But I saw Fortune last week, and he never mentioned your coming,' pursued Mr Nutley, mystified.

'No, I daresay he didn't; in point of fact, he knew nothing about it until I turned up here.'

'What, you didn't let the servants know?'

'No, I didn't,' Chase entered suddenly upon a definite dislike of Mr Nutley. He felt a relief as soon as he had realised it; he felt more settled and definite in his mind, cleared of the cobwebs of a vague uneasiness. Nutley was too inquisitorial, too managing altogether. Blackboys was his own to come to, if he chose. Still his own – for another month.

'What on earth have you got there?' said Nutley peering at a crumpled bunch that Chase carried in his hand.

'Butcher-boys,' replied Chase.

'They're wild orchids,' said Mr Nutley, after peering a little closer. 'Why do you call them butcher-boys?'

'That's what the children call them,' mumbled Chase, 'I don't know them by any other name. Ugly things, anyhow,' he added, flinging them away.

'Soft, soft,' said Nutley to himself, tapping his forehead as he walked on alone.

He proceeded towards the house. Queer of Chase, to come back like that, without a word to anyone. What about that business of his in Wolverhampton? He seemed to be less anxious about that now. As though he couldn't leave matters to Nutley and Farebrother, Solicitors and Estate Agents, without slipping back to see to things himself! Spying, no less. Queer, sly, silent fellow, mooning about the park, carrying wild orchids. 'Butcher-boys' he had called them. What children had he been consorting with, to learn that country name? There had been an odd look in his eye, too, when Nutley had come upon him, as though he were vexed at being seen, and would have liked to slink off in the opposite direction. Queer, too, that he should have made no reference to the approaching sale. He might at least have asked whether the estate office had received any private applications. But Nutley had already noticed that he took very little interest in the subject of the sale. An unsatisfactory employer, except in so far as he never interfered; it was unsatisfactory never to know whether one's employer approved of what was being done or not.

And under his irritability was another grievance: the suspicion that Chase was a dark horse. The solicitor had always marked down Blackboys as a ripe plum to fall into his hands when old Miss Chase died – obstinate, opinionated, old Phillida Chase. He had never considered the heir at all. It was almost as though he looked upon himself as the heir – the impatient heir, hostile and vindictive towards the coveted inheritance.

Nutley reached the house, where, his hand upon the latch of the little wooden gate, he was checked by a padlock within the hasp. He was irritated, and shook the latch roughly. He thought that the quiet house, safe behind its gate and its sleeping moat, smiled and mocked him. Then, more sensibly, he pulled the bell beside the gate, and waited till the tinkle inside the house brought Fortune hurrying to open.

'What's this affair, eh, Fortune?' said Nutley with false good humour, pointing to the padlock.

'The padlock, sir? That's there by Mr Chase's orders,' replied Fortune demurely.

'Mr Chase's orders?' repeated Mr Nutley, not believing his own ears.

'Mr Chase has been very much annoyed, sir, by motoring parties coming to look over the house, and making free of the place.'

'But they may have been intending purchasers!' Mr Nutley almost shrieked, touched upon the raw.

'Yes, sir, they all had orders to view. All except one party, that is, that came yesterday. Mr Chase turned them away, sir.'

'Turned them away?'

'Yes, sir. They came in a big car. Mr Chase talked to them himself over the gate. He had the key in his pocket. No, sir, he wouldn't unlock it. He said that if they wanted to buy the house they would have the opportunity of doing so at the auction. Yes, sir, they seemed considerably annoyed. They said they had come from London on purpose. They said they should have thought that if anyone had a house to sell, he would have been only too glad to show parties over it, order or no order, they said, especially if the house was so unsaleable, two hours by train from London and not up to date in any way. Mr Chase said, very curt-like, that if they wanted an up-to-date house, Blackboys was not likely to suit them. He just lifted his cap, and wished them good evening, and came back by himself into the house, with the key still in his pocket, and the car drove away. Very insolent sort of people they were, sir, I must say.'

Fortune delivered himself of this recital in a tone that was a strange compound of respect, reticence, and a secret relish. During its telling he had followed Mr Nutley's progress into the house, until they arrived in the panelled library where the coral-coloured tulips reared themselves so luminously against the sobriety of the books and of the oak. Mr Nutley noticed them, because it was easier to pass a comment on a bowl of flowers than upon Chase's inexplicable behaviour.

'Yes, sir, very pretty; Mr Chase puts them there,' said Fortune, with the satisfaction of one who adds a final touch to a suggestive sketch.

'Shouldn't have thought he'd ever looked at a flower in his life,' muttered Nutley.

He deposited his bag on the table, and turned to the butler.

'Quite between you and me, Fortune, what you tell me surprises me very much – about the visiting parties, I mean. And the padlock. Um – the padlock. I always thought Mr Chase very *quiet*; but you don't, do you, think him *soft*?'

Fortune knew that Nutley enjoyed saying that. He remembered how he had caught Chase, the day before, studying bumbledories on the low garden wall; but he withheld the bumbledories from Mr Nutley.

'It wouldn't be unnatural, sir,' he submitted, 'if Mr Chase had a feeling about Blackboys being in the market?'

'Feeling? Pooh!' said Mr. Nutley. He said 'Pooh!' again to reassure himself, because he knew that Fortune, sentimental and shrewd, had hit the nail on the head. 'He'd never set eyes on Blackboys until three weeks ago. Besides, what could he do with the place except put it in the market? Tell me that! Absurd!'

He was sorting papers out of his black bag. Their neat stiffness gave him the reassuring sense of being here among matters which he competently understood. This was his province. He would have said, had he been asked a day earlier, that it was Chase's province too. Now he was not so sure.

'Sentimentality!' he snorted. It was his most damning criticism.

Chase's pipe was lying on the table beside the tulips; he picked it up and regarded it with a mixture of reproach and indignation. It reposed mutely in his hand.

'Ridiculous!' said Nutley, dashing it down again as though that settled the matter.

'The people round here have taken to him wonderful,' put in Fortune.

Nutley looked sharply at him; he stood by the table, demure, grizzled, and perfectly respectful.

'Why, has he been round talking to the people?'

'A good deal, sir, among the tenants like. Wonderful how he gets on with them, for a city-bred man. I don't hold with city breeding, myself. Will you be staying to luncheon, sir?'

'Yes,' replied Mr Nutley, preoccupied and profoundly suspicious.

7

Suspicious of Chase, though he couldn't justify his suspicion. Tested even by the severity of the solicitor's standards, Chase's behaviour and conversation during luncheon were irreproachable. No sooner had he entered the house than he began briskly talking of business. Yet Nutley continued to eye him as one who beneath reasonable words and a bland demeanour nourishes a secret and a joke; a silent and deeply buried understanding. He talked sedately enough, keeping to the subject even with a certain rigour – acreage, rents, building possibilities; and intelligent interest. Still, Nutley could have sworn there was irony in it. Irony from Chase? Weedy, irritable little man, Chase. Not today though; not irritable today. In a good temper. (Ironical?) Playing the host, sitting at the head of the refectory table while Nutley sat at the side. Naturally. Very cordial, very open-handed with the port. Quite at home in the dining room, ordering his dog to a corner; and in the library too, with his pipes and tobacco strewn about. How long ago was it, since Nutley was warning him not to slip on the polished boards?

Then a stroll round the garden, Chase with crumbs in his pocket for the peacocks.

When they saw him, two or three hopped majestically down from the parapet, and came stalking towards him. Accustomed to crumbs evidently. 'You haven't had them destroyed, then?' said Nutley, eyeing them with mistrust and disapproval, and Chase laughed without answering. Up the centre walk of the garden, and back by the herbaceous borders along the walls: lilac, wisteria, patches of tulips, colonies of iris. All the while Chase never deviated from the topic of selling. He pointed out the house, folded in the hollow down the gentle slope of the garden. 'Not bad, for those who like it. Thirty thousand for the house, I think you said?' 'Then why the devil,' Nutley wanted to say, but refrained from saying, 'do you turn away people who come in a big car?' They strolled down the slope, Chase breaking from the lilac bushes an armful of the heavy plumes.

He seemed to do it with an unknowing gesture, as though he couldn't keep his hands off flowers, and then to be embarrassed on discovering in his arms the wealth that he had gathered. It was as though he had kept an adequate guard over his tongue while allowing his gestures to escape him. He took Nutley round to the entrance, where the station cab was waiting, and unlocked the gate with the key he carried in his pocket.

'You go back to Wolverhampton tomorrow?' said Mr Nutley, preparing to depart.

'That's it,' replied Chase. Did he look sly, or didn't he?

'All the arrangements will be made by the end of next week,' said Nutley severely.

'That's splendid!' replied Chase. Nutley, as he was driven away, had a last glimpse of him, leaning still against the gate-post, vaguely holding the lilac.

8

Chase didn't go back to Wolverhampton. He knew that it was his duty to go, but he stayed on at Blackboys. Not only that, but he sent no letter or telegram in explanation of his continued absence. He simply stayed where he was, callous, and supremely happy. By no logic could he have justified his behaviour; by no effort of the imagination could he, a fortnight earlier, have conceived such behaviour as proceeding from his well-ordered creeds. He stayed on, through the early summer days that throughout all their hours preserved the clarity of dawn. Like a child strayed into the realms of delight, he was stupefied by the enchantment of sun and shadow. He remained for hours gazing in a silly beatitude at the large patches of sunlight that lay on the grass, at the depths of the shadows that melted into the profundity of the woods. In the mornings he woke early, and leaning at the open window gave himself over to the dews, to the young glinting sunshine, and to the birds. What a babble of birds! He couldn't distinguish their notes – only to the cuckoo, the woodpigeon, and the distant crow of a cock could he put a name. The fluffy tits, blue and yellow, hopping among the apple branches, were to him as nameless as they were lovely. He knew, theoretically, that the birds did sing when day was breaking; the marvellous thing was, not that they should be singing, but that he, Chase, should be awake and in the country to hear them sing. No one knew that he was awake, and he had all a shy man's pleasure in seclusion. No one knew what he was doing; no one was spying on him; he was quite free and unobserved in this clean-washed, untenanted, waking world. Down in the woods only the small animals and the birds were stirring. There was the rustle of a mouse under dead leaves. It was too early for even the farm people to be about. Chase and the natural citizens between them had it all their own way. (Nutley wore a black coat and carried a black shiny bag, but Nutley knew nothing of the dawn.) Then he clothed himself, and, passing out of the house unperceived with Thane, since there was no one to perceive them, wandered in the sparkling fields. There was by now no angle from which he was not familiar with the house, whether he considered the dreamy roofs from the crest of the hill or the huddle of the murrey-coloured buildings from across the distance of the surrounding pastures. No thread of smoke rose slim and wavering from a chimney but he could trace it down to its hearthstone. No window glittered but he could name the room it lit. Nor was there any tenderness of light whose change he had not observed, whether of the morning, cool and fluty; or of the richer evening, profound and venerable, that sank upon the ruby brickwork, the glaucous moat, and the breasts of the peacocks in the garden; or of the ethereal moonlight, a secret that he kept, inviolate almost from himself, in the shyest recesses of his soul.

For at the centre of all was always the house, that mothered the farms and accepted the homage of the garden. The house was at the heart of all things; the cycle of husbandry might revolve – tillage to growth, and growth to harvest – more necessary, more permanent, perhaps, more urgent; but like a woman gracious, humorous, and dominant, the house remained quiet at the centre. To part the house and the lands, or to consider them as separate, would be no less than parting the soul and the body. The house *was* the soul; did contain and guard the soul as in a casket; the lands were England, Saxon as they could be, and if the house were at the heart of the land, then the soul of the house must indeed be at the heart and root of England, and, once arrived at the soul of the house, you might fairly claim to have pierced to the soul of England. Grave, gentle, encrusted with tradition, embossed with legend, simple and proud, ample and maternal. Not sensational. Not arresting. There was nothing about the house or the country to startle; it was, rather, a charm that enticed, insidious as a track through a wood, or a path lying across fields and curving away from sight over the skyline, leading the unwary wanderer deeper and deeper into the bosom of the country.

He knew the sharp smell of cut grass, and the wash of the dew round his ankles. He knew the honing of a scythe, the clang of a forge and the roaring of its bellows, the rasp of a saw cutting through wood and the resinous scent of the sawdust. He knew the tap of a woodpecker on a tree trunk, and the mid-day murmur, most amorous, most sleepy, of the pigeons among the beeches. He knew the contented buzz of a bee as it closed down upon a flower, and the bitter shrill of the grasshopper along the hedgerows. He knew the squirt of milk jetting into the pails, and the drowsy stir in the byres. He knew the marvellous brilliance of a petal in the sun, its fibrous transparency, like the cornelian-coloured transparency of a woman's fingers held over a strong light. He associated these sights, and the infinitesimal small sounds composing the recurrent melody, with the meals prepared for him, the salads and cold chicken, the draughts of cider, and abundance of fresh humble fruit, until it seemed to him that all senses were gratified severally and harmoniously, as well out in the open as in the cool dusk within the house.

He liked to rap with his stick upon the door of a farmhouse, and to be admitted with a 'Why! Mr Chase!' by a smiling woman into the passage, smelling of recent soap and water on the tiles; to be ushered into the sitting room, hideous, pretentious, and strangely meaningless, furnished always with the cottage piano, the Turkey carpet, and the plant in a bright gilt basket-pot. The light in these rooms always struck Chase as being particularly unmerciful. But he learnt that he must sit patient, while the farmer was summoned, and the rest of the household too, and sherry in a decanter and a couple of glasses were produced from a sideboard, at whatever hour Chase's visit might chance to fall, be it even at eight in the morning, which it very often was. That lusty hospitality permitted no refusal of the sherry, though Chase might have preferred, instead of the burning stuff, a glass of fresh milk after his walk across the dews. He must sit and sip the sherry, responding to the social efforts of the farmer's wife and daughters (the latter always coy, always would be up to date), while the farmer was content to leave this indoor portion of the entertainment to his womenfolk, contributing nothing himself but 'Another glass, Mr Chase?' or the offer of a cigar, and the creak of his leather gaiters as he trod across the room. But presently, Chase knew, when the conversation became really impossibly stilted, he might without incivility suggest that he mustn't keep the farmer any longer from his daily business, and, after shaking hands all round with the ladies, might take his cap and follow his host out into the yard, where men pitchforked the sodden litter out into the midden in the centre of the yard, and the slow cattle lurched one behind the other from the sheds, turning themselves unprompted in the familiar direction. Here, Chase might be certain he would not be embarrassed by having undue notice taken of him. The farmer here was a greater man than he. Chase liked to follow round meekly, and the more he was neglected the better he was pleased. Then he and the farmer together would tramp across the acres, silent for the most part, but inwardly contented, although when the farmer broke the silence it was only to grunt out some phrase of complaint, either at the poverty of that year's yield, or the dearth or abundance of rabbits, or to remark, kicking at a clod of loam, 'Soggy, soggy! The land's not yet forgotten the rains we had in February,' thus endowing the land with a personality actual and rancorous, more definite to Chase than the personalities of the yeomen, whom he could distinguish apart by their appearance perhaps, but certainly not by their opinions, their preoccupations, or their gestures. They were natural features rather than men – trees or boles, endowed with speech and movement indeed, but preserving the same unity, the same hodden unwieldiness, that was integral with the landscape. There was one old hedger in particular who, maundering over his business of lop and top, or grubbing among the ditches, had grown as gnarled and horny as an ancient root, and was scarcely distinguishable till you came right upon him, when his little brown dog flew out from the hedge and barked; and there was another chubby old man, a dealer in fruit, who drove about the country, a long ladder swaying out of the back of his cart. This old man was intimate with every orchard of the countryside, whether apple, cherry, damson, or plum, and could tell you the harvest gathered in bushel measures for any year within his memory; but although all fruits came within his province, the apples had his especial affection, and he never referred to them save by the personal pronouns, 'Ah, Winter Queening,' he would say, 'she's a grand bearer,' or 'King of the Pippins, he's a fine fellow,' and for Chase, whom he had taken under his protection, he would always produce some choice specimen from his pocket with a confidential air, although, as he never failed to observe, 'May wasn't the time for apples.' Let Mr Chase only wait till the autumn – he would show him what a Ribston or a Blenheim ought to be; 'But I shan't be here in the autumn, Caleb,' Chase would say, and the old man would jerk his head sagely and reply as he whipped up the pony, 'Trees with old roots isn't so easily thrown over,' and in the parable that he only half understood Chase found an obscure comfort.

These were his lane-made friendships. He knew the man who cut withies by the brook; he knew the gang and the six great shining horses that dragged away the chained and fallen trees upon an enormous wain; he knew the boys who went after moorhen's eggs; he knew the kingfisher that was always ambushed somewhere near the bridge; he knew the cheery woman who had an idiot child, and a husband accursed of bees. 'Bees? No, my husband couldn't never go near bees. He squashed up too many of them when he was a lad, and bees never forget. Squashed 'em up, so, in his hand. Just temper. Now if three bees stung him together he'd die. Oh, surely, Mr Chase, sir. We went down into Sussex once, on a holiday, and the bees there knew him at once and were after him. Wonderful thing it is, the sense beasts have got. And memory! Beasts never forget, beasts don't.'

And always there was the reference to the sale, and the regrets, that were never impertinent and never ruffled so much as the fringes of Chase's pride. The women were readier with these regrets than the men; they started off with unthinking sympathy, while the men shuffled and coughed, and traced with their toe the pattern of the carpet, but presently, when alone with Chase, took advantage of the women's prerogative in breaking the ice, to revive the subject; and always Chase, to get himself out of a conversation which he felt to be fraught with awkwardness – the awkwardness of reserved men trespassing upon the grounds of secret and personal feeling – would parry with his piteous jest of being himself under notice to quit.

9

When the inventory men came, Chase suffered. They came with bags, ledgers, pencils; they were brisk and efficient, and Chase fled them from room to room. They soon put him down as oddly peevish, not knowing that they had committed the extreme offence of disturbing his dear privacy. In their eyes, after all, they were there as his employees, carrying out his orders. The foreman even went out of his way to be appreciative, 'Nice lot of stuff you have there, sir,' he said to Chase, when his glance first travelled over the dim velvets and gilt of the furniture in the Long Gallery, 'should do well under the hammer.' Chase stood beside him, seeing the upholstered depths of velvets and damasks, like ripe fruits, heavily fringed and tasselled; the plasterwork of the diapered ceiling; the fairytale background of the tapestry, and the reflections of the cloudy mirrors. Into this room also he had put bowls of flowers, not knowing that the inventory men were coming so soon. 'Nice lot of stuff you have here, sir,' said the foreman.

Chase remembered how often, representing his insurance company, he had run a casual and assessing eye over other people's possessions.

The inventory men worked methodically through the house. Ground floor, staircase, landing, passage, first floor. Everything was ticketed and checked. Chase miserably avoided their hearty communicativeness. He skulked in the sitting room downstairs, or, when he was driven out of that, took his cap and walked away from the house that surrounded him now with the grief of a wistful reproach. He knew that he would be well-advised to leave, yet he delayed from day to day; he suffered, but he stayed on, impotently watching the humbling and the desecration of the house. Then he took to going amongst the men when they were at their work, 'What might be the value of a thing like this?' he would ask, tapping picture, cabinet, or chair with a contemptuous finger; and, when told, he would express surprise that anyone could be fool enough to pay such a price for an object so unserviceable, worm-eaten, or insecure. He would stand by, derisively sucking the top of his cane, while clerk and foreman checked and inscribed. Sometimes he would pick up some object just entered, a blue porcelain bowl, or whatever it might be, turn it between his hands, examine it, and set it back on the window ledge with a shrug of the shoulders. There were no flowers in the rooms now, nor did he leave his pipes and tobacco littering the tables, but kept them hidden away in a drawer. There had been places, intimate to him, where he had grown accustomed to put his things, knowing he would find them there on his return; but he now broke himself of this weakness with a wrench. It hurt, and he was grim about it. In the evenings he sat solitary in a stiff room, without the companionship of those familiar things in their familiar niches. Towards Fortune his manner changed, and he appeared to take a pleasure in speaking callously, even harshly, of the forthcoming sale; but the old servant saw through him. When people came now to visit the house, he took them over every corner of it himself, deploring its lack of convenience, pointing out the easy remedy, and vaunting the advantage of its architectural perfection, 'Quoted in every book on the subject,' he would say, 'a perfect specimen of domestic Elizabethan,' (this phrase he had picked up from an article in an architectural journal), 'complete in every detail, down to the window fastenings; you wouldn't find another like it, in the length and breadth of England.' The people to whom he said these things looked at him curiously; he spoke in a shrill, eager voice, and they thought he must be very anxious to sell. 'Hard-up, no doubt,' they said as they went away. Others said, 'He probably belongs to a distant branch of the family, and doesn't care.'

10

After the inventory men, the dealers. Cigars, paunches, check waistcoats, signet rings. Insolent plump hands thumbing the velvets; shiny lips pushed out in disparagement, while small eyes twinkled with concupiscence. Chase grew to know them well. Yet he taught himself to banter even with the dealers, to pretend his excessive boredom with the whole uncongenial business. He advertised his contempt for the possessions that circumstances had thrust on him; they could and should, he let it be understood, affect him solely through their marketable value. The house itself – he quoted Nutley, to the dealers not to the people who came in view – 'Small rooms, dark passages, no bathrooms, no electric light.' He said these things often and loudly, and laughed after he had said them as though he had uttered a witticism. The dealers laughed with him, politely, but they thought him a little wild, and from time to time cast at him a glance of slight surprise.

All this while he sent no letter to Wolverhampton. He got one letter from his office, a typewritten letter, considerate and long-suffering, addressed to P. Chase, Esq., at the foot (he was accustomed to seeing himself referred to as 'our Mr Chase' by his firm – anyhow they hadn't ferreted out the Peregrine), suggesting that, although they quite understood that private affairs of importance were detaining him, he might perhaps for their guidance indicate an approximate date for his return. He reflected vaguely that they were treating him very decently; and dropped the letter into the wastepaper basket.

11

He saw, however, that he would soon have to go. He clung on, but the sale was imminent; red and black posters appeared on all the cottages; and larger, redder, and blacker posters announced the sale, 'By order of Peregrine Chase, Esq.,' of 'the unique collection of antique furniture, tapestries, pictures, and contents of the mansion,' and in types of varying size detailed these contents, so that Chase could see, flaunting upon walls, trees, and gateposts, when he wandered out, the soulless dates and the auctioneer's bombast that advertised for others the quality of his possessions.

An illustrated booklet was likewise published. Nutley gave him a copy. 'This quite unique sixteenth-century residence'; 'the most original panelling and plasterwork'; 'the moat and contemporary outbuildings'; 'the old-world garden' – Chase fluttered over the pages, and rage seized him by the throat. 'Nicely got up, don't you think?' Nutley said complacently.

Chase took the booklet away with him, up into the gallery. He always liked the gallery, because it was long, low, deserted, and so glowingly ornate; and more peaceful than any of the other rooms in the whole peaceful house. When he went there with the booklet in his hand that evening, he sat quite still for a time while the hush that his entrance had disturbed settled down again upon the room and its occupant. A latticed rectangle of deep gold lay across the boards, the last sunlight of the day. Chase turned over the leaves of the book. 'The Oak Parlour, an apartment 20 ft. by 25 ft., partially panelled in linen-fold in a state of the finest preservation.' Was that his library? It couldn't be, so accurate, so precise? Why, the room was living! Through the windows one saw up the garden, and saw the peacocks perched on the low wall, one heard their cry as they flew up into the cedars for the night; and in the evening, in that room, the fir cones crackled on the hearth, the dry wood kindled, and the room began to smell ever so slightly of the clean, acrid wood smoke that never quite left it, but remained clinging even when the next day the windows were open and the warm breeze fanned into the room. He had known all that about it, although he hadn't known it was twenty foot by twenty-five. He hadn't known that the panelling against which he had been accustomed to set his bowl of coral tulips was called linen-fold.

He was an ignorant fellow; he hadn't known; he didn't know anything even now; the sooner he went back to Wolver-hampton the better.

He turned over another page of the booklet. 'The Great Staircase and Armorial Window, (cir. 1584) with coats of arms of the families of Chase, Dacre, Medlicott, and Cullinbroke,' – the window whose gaudiness always seemed to attract a pea-cock to parade in rivalry on the outer ledge, like the first day he had come to Blackboys; but why had they given everything such high-sounding names? The 'Great Staircase,' for instance; it was never called that, but only 'the staircase,' nor was it particularly great, only wide and polished and leisurely. He supposed Nutley was responsible, or was it Farebrother? Farebrother who was so kindly, and might have wanted to salve Chase's feelings by appealing to his vanity through the splendour of his property?

What a fool he was; of course, neither Nutley nor Fare-brother gave a thought to his feelings, but only to the expedi-ency of selling the house.

He turned the pages further. 'The Long Gallery,' – here, at least, they had not tried to improve upon the usual name – 'a spacious apartment running the whole length of the upper floor, 100 ft. by 30 ft. wide, sumptuously ornamented in the Italian style of the sixteenth century, with mullioned heraldic

'When does he think he's coming back? The sale takes place next week,' grumbled Nutley.

It was nearly midsummer; the heat-haze wickered above the ground, and the garden was tumultuous with butterflies and flowers.

'It seems a pity to think of Mr Chase missing all this fine weather,' Fortune remarked.

Nutley had no affection whatever for Fortune; he possessed the knack of making remarks to which he could not reasonably take exception, but which contrived slightly to irritate him.

'I daresay he's getting the fine weather where he is,' he replied curtly.

'Ah, but in towns it isn't the same thing; when he's got his own garden here, and all,' said Fortune, not yielding to Nutley, who merely shrugged, and started talking about the sale in a sharp voice.

He was in his element, Chase once dismissed from his mind. He came up to Blackboys nearly every day, quite unnecessarily, giving every detail his attention, fawning upon anyone who seemed a likely purchaser for the house, gossiping with the dealers who now came in large numbers, and accepting their cigars with a 'Well, I don't mind if I do – bit of a strain, you know, all this – the responsibility, and so on.' He had the acquisitiveness of a magpie, for scraps of sale-room gossip. Dealers ticking off items in their catalogues, men in green baize aprons shifting furniture, the front door standing permanently open to all comers, were all a source of real gratification to him; while in the number of motors that waited under the shade of the trees he took a personal pride. He rubbed his hands with pleasure over the coming and going, and at the crunch of fresh wheels on the gravel. Chase's ridiculous little padlock on the wooden gate – there wasn't much trace of that now! Front door and back door were open, the summer breeze wandering gently between

windows, overmantel of sculptured marble, rich plastered ceiling,' here he raised his eyes and let them stray down the length of the gallery; the rectangle of sunlight had grown deeper and more luminous; the blocks of shadow in the corners had spread, the velvet chairs against the tapestry had merged and become yet more fruity; they were like split figs, like plums, like ripe mulberries; the colour of the room was as luxuriant as the spilling out of a cornucopia. Chase became aware that Fortune was standing beside him.

'Mr Nutley asked me to tell you, sir, that he couldn't wait any longer, but that he'll be here again tomorrow.'

Chase blushed and stammered, as he always did when someone took him by surprise, and as he more particularly did when that someone happened to be one of his own servants. Then he saw tears standing in the old butler's eyes. He thought angrily to himself that the man was as soft-hearted as an old woman.

'Seen this little book, Fortune?' he inquired, holding it out towards him.

'Oh, sir!' exclaimed the butler, turning aside.

'Well, what's the matter? What's the matter?' said Chase, in his most irritable tone.

He got up and moved away. He went out into the garden, troubled and disquieted by the excessive tumult in his soul. He gazed down upon the mellow roofs and chimneys, veiled in a haze of blue smoke; upon all the beauty that had given him peace and content; but far from deriving comfort now he felt himself provoked by a fresh anguish, impotent and yet rebellious, a weak fury, an irresolute insubordination. Schemes, that his practical sense told him were fantastically futile, kept dashing across his mind. He would tell Fortune to shut the door in everybody's face, more especially Nutley's. He would destroy the bridge across the moat. He would sulk inside his house, admitting no one; he and his house, alone, allied against rapacity. Fortune and the few other servants might desert him if they chose; he would cook for himself, he would dust, he would think it an honour to dust; and suddenly the contrast between the picture of himself with a duster in his hand, and of himself striking at the bridge with a pickaxe, caused him to laugh out loud, a laugh bitter and tormented, that could never have issued from his throat in the Wolverhampton days. He wished that he were back in those days, again the conscientious drudge, earning enough to keep himself in decent lodgings (not among brocades and fringes, or plumed and canopied beds, not in the midst of this midsummer loveliness, that laid the hands more gentle and more detaining than the hands of any woman about his heart, not this old dignity that touched his pride), and he stared down upon the roofs of the house lying cupped in its hollow, resentful of the vision that had thus opened out as though by treachery at a turning of his drab existence, yet unable to sustain a truly resentful or angry thought, by reason of the tenderness that melted him, and the mute plea of his inheritance, that, scorning any device more theatrical, quietly relied upon its simple beauty as its only mediator.

12

Mr Nutley was considerably relieved when he heard that Chase had gone back to Wolverhampton. From being negligible, Chase had lately become a slightly inconvenient presence at Blackboys; not that he ever criticised or interfered with the arrangements that Nutley made, but Nutley felt vaguely that he watched everything and registered internal comments; yes, although not a very sensitive chap, perhaps – he hadn't time for that – Nutley had become aware that very little eluded Chase's observation. It was odd, and rather annoying, that in spite of his taciturnity and his shy manner, Chase should so contrive to make himself felt. Any of the people on the estate, who had spoken with him more than once or twice, had a liking and a respect for him. Perhaps, Nutley consoled himself, it was thanks to tradition quite as much as to Chase's personality, and he permitted himself a little outburst against the tradition he hated, envied, and scorned.

Now that Chase had gone back to Wolverhampton, Nutley arrived more aggressively at Blackboys, rang the bell louder, made more demands on Fortune, and bustled everybody about the place.

The first time he came there in the owner's absence the dog met him in the hall, stretching himself as though just awakened from sleep, coming forward with his nails clicking on the boards.

'He misses his master,' said Fortune compassionately.

Nutley thought, with discomfort, that the whole place missed Chase. There were traces of him everywhere – the obverse of his handwriting on the pad of blotting paper in the library, his stick in the hall, and some of his clothes in a pile on the bed in his bedroom.

'Yes, Mr Chase left a good many of his things behind,' said Fortune when consulted.

them and winnowing the shreds of straw that trailed about the hall, and in the passage beyond; and anyone who had finished inspecting the house might pass into the garden by the back door, to stroll up the central walk, till Nutley, looking out of an upper floor window, taking upon himself the whole credit, and full of a complacent satisfaction, thought that the place had the appearance of a garden party.

A country sale! It was one that would set two counties talking, one that would attract all the biggest swells from London (Wertheimer, Durlacher, Duveen, Partridge, they had all been already, taking notes), such a collection didn't often come under the hammer – no, by jove, it didn't! And Nutley, reading for the fiftieth time the name 'Nutley, Farebrother and Co., Estate Agents and Solicitors,' at the foot of the poster, reflected how that name would gain in fame and lustre by the association. Not that Farebrother, not that Co., had been allowed many fingers in the pie; he, Nutley, had done it all; it was *his* show, *his* ewe-lamb; he would have snapped the head off anyone who had dared to claim a share, or scorned them with a single glance.

He wondered to whom the house itself would ultimately fall. He had received several offers for it, but none of them had reached the reserve figure of thirty thousand. The dealers, of course, would make a ring for the furniture, the tapestries, and the pictures, and would doubtless resell them to the new owner of the house at an outrageous profit. Nutley had his eye on a Brazilian as a very probable purchaser; not only had he called at the estate office himself for all possible particulars, but on a second occasion he had brought his son and his daughter with him, exotic birds brilliantly descending upon the country solicitor's office. They had come in a white Rolls-Royce, which had immediately compelled Nutley's disapproving respect; it had a negro chauffeur on the box, the silver statuette of a nymph with streaming hair on the bonnet, and a spray of orchids in a silver and crystal vase inside. The Brazilian himself was an unpretentious cattle magnate, with a quick, clipped manner, and a wrinkled face the colour of a coffee bean; he might be the purveyor of dollars, but he wasn't the showy one; the ostentation of the family had passed into the children. These were in their early twenties, spoilt and fretful; the tyrants of their widowed father, who listened to all their remarks with an indulgent smile. Nutley, who had never in the whole of his life seen anything like them, tried to make himself believe that he couldn't decide which was the more offensive, but, secretly, he was much impressed. 'Plenty of bounce, anyway,' he reflected, observing the son, his pearl-grey suit over admirably waisted stays, his black hair swept back from his brow, and shining like the flanks of a wet seal, his lean hands weighted with fat platinum rings, his walk that slightly swayed, as though the syncopated rhythm of the plantations had passed for ever into his blood; and, observing him, the strangest shadow of envy passed across the shabby little solicitor in the presence of such lackadaisical youth... The daughter, more languid and more subtly insolent, so plump that she seemed everywhere cushioned: her tiny hands had no knuckles, but only dimples, and everything about her was round, from the single pearls on her fingers to the toecaps of her patent leather shoes. Clearly the father had offered Blackboys to the pair as an additional toy. They were as taken with it as their deliberately unenthusiastic manner would permit them to betray; and Nutley guessed that sufficient sulks on the part of the daughter would quickly induce the widower to increase his offer of twenty-five thousand by the necessary five. Up to the present he had held firm, a business convention which Nutley was ready tacitly to accept. He had reported the visit to Chase, but Chase (the unaccountable) hadn't taken much interest. Since then he had seen the brother and sister

58

several times wandering over the house and garden, and this he took to be a promising sign. The father he hadn't seen again, but that didn't distress him: the insolent pair were the ones who counted.

13

Only two days remained. Chase had sent for his clothes, and had enclosed a note for Nutley in his letter to Fortune: 'Press of business' prevented him from returning to Blackboys, but he was content to leave everything in Nutley's hands, etc. Polite enough. Nutley read the note, standing in the gallery which had been cleared in preparation for the sale. (It was, he thought, a stroke of genius to hold the sale in the house itself – to display the furniture in its own surroundings, instead of in the dreary frame of an auction room. That would make very little difference to the dealers, of course, who knew the intrinsic value; but from the stray buyers, the amateurs who would be after the less important things, it might mean anything up to an extra twenty-five per cent.) He was alone in the gallery, for it was not yet ten o'clock, and he maliciously wondered what Chase's feelings would be if he could see the room now, the baize-covered tables on trestle legs, the auctioneer's desk and high chair, the rows of cane chairs arranged as though in a theatre, the choicest pieces of furniture grouped behind cords at the further end of the room, like animals awaiting slaughter in a pen. The little solicitor was from time to time startled by the stab of malice that thought of Chase evoked; he was startled now. He clapped his hand over his mouth – to suppress an ejaculation, or a grin? – and glanced round the gallery. It was empty but for the lean dog, who sat with his tail curled like a whiplash round his haunches, and who might have come down out of the tapestry, gravely regarding Nutley. The lean dog, scenting disruption, had trailed about the house for days like a haunted soul, and Nutley had fallen into the habit of saying to him, with a jocularity oddly peppered by venom, 'I'll put you into the sale as an extra item, spindle-shanks.'

Dimly, it gratified him to insult Chase through Chase's dog.

People began to filter in. They wandered about, looking at things and consulting their catalogues; Nutley, who examined them stealthily and with as much self-consciousness as if he had been the owner, discriminated nicely between the *bona fide* buyers and those who came out of idle curiosity. (Chase had already recognised the mentality that seizes upon any pretext for penetrating into another man's house; if as far as his bedroom, so much the better.) Nutley might as well have returned to his office since here there was no longer anything for him to do, but he lingered, with the satisfaction of an impresario. Could he but have stood at the front door, to receive the people as the cars rolled up at intervals! Hospitable and welcoming phrases came springing to his lips, and his hands spread themselves urbanely, the palms outwards. No sharpness in his manner! None of the chilblained acerbity that kept him always on the defensive! Nothing but honey and suavity! 'Walk in, walk in, ladies and gentlemen! No entrance fee in my peep show. Twenty years I had to wait for the old woman to die; I fixed my eye on her when she was sixty, but she clung on till she was over eighty; then she went. It's all in my hands now. Walk in, walk in, ladies and gentlemen; walk upstairs; the show's going to begin.'

It was very warm. Really an exceptional summer. If the weather held for another two days, it would improve the attendance at the sale. London people would come (Nutley had the sudden idea of running a special). Even now, picnic parties were dotted about, under the trees beside their motors. No wonder that they were glad to exchange burning pavements against fresh grass for a day. Chase – Chase wouldn't like the litter they left. Bits of paper, bottles and tins. He wouldn't say anything; he never did; that was exactly what made him so disconcerting; but he would look, and his nose would curl. But Chase was safely away, while the picnics took place under his trees, and women in their light summer dresses strolled about in his garden and pointed with their parasols at his house. Nutley saw them from the windows. For the first time since he remembered the place, the parapet of the central walk was bare of peacocks; they had taken refuge indignantly in the cedars, where they could be heard screeching. He remembered Chase, feeding them with bits of bread from his pocket. He remembered old Miss Chase, wagging her finger at him, and saying 'Ah, Nutley,' (she had always called him by his surname, like a man), 'you want to deprive an old maid of her children; it's too bad of you!'

But the Chases were gone, both of them, and no Chases remained, but those who stared sadly from their frames, where they stood propped against the wall ready to be carried into the sale room.

14

June the twenty-first. The day of the sale. Midsummer day. Nutley's day. He arrived early at the house, and met at the door Colonel Stanforth, who had walked across the park, and who considered the solicitor's umbrella with amusement. 'Afraid it will rain, Nutley? Look at that blue sky, not a cloud, not even a white one.' They entered the house together, Stanforth rubicund and large, Nutley noticeably spare in the black coat that enveloped him like a sheath. 'Might be an undertaker's mute,' Stanforth commented inwardly. 'Isn't Farebrother coming up today?' he asked aloud. 'Oh, yes, I daresay he'll look in later,' Nutley answered, implying as clearly as possible by his tone that it was not of the slightest importance whether his partner looked in or not.

'Well, there aren't many people about yet,' said Stanforth, rubbing his hands vigorously together. 'What about your Brazilians, eh? Are they going to put in an appearance? Chase, I hear, is still in Wolverhampton.'

'Yes,' answered Nutley, 'we shan't see much of *him*.'

'Of course, there was no necessity for him to come, but it's odd of him to take so little interest, don't you think? Odd, I mean, as he seemed to like staying in the place, and to have got on so remarkably well with all the people around. Not that I saw anything of him when he was here. An unneighbourly sort of fellow, I should think. But to hear some of the people talk about him, by Gad, I was quite sorry he couldn't settle down here as squire.'

'As you say, there was no necessity for him to come to the sale,' said Nutley, frigidly ignoring the remainder of Stanforth's remarks.

'No, but if I'd been he, I don't think I could have kept away, all the same.'

Nutley went off, saying he had things to see to. On the landing he met the butler with Thane slouching disconsolately after him.

'You'll see that that dog's shut up, Fortune,' he snapped at him.

An air of suspense hung over everything. The sale was announced to begin at midday, because the London train arrived shortly after eleven, but before then the local attendance poured in, and many people drove up who had not previously been seen at the house, their business being with the lands or the farms: farmers in their gigs, tiptoeing awkwardly and apologetically on the polished boards of the hall while their horses were led away into the stable-yard, and there were many of the gentry too, who came in waggonettes or pony-traps. Nutley, watching and prying everywhere, observed the arrival of the latter with mixed feelings. On the one hand their presence increased the crush, but on the other hand he did not for a moment suppose they had come to buy. They came in families, shy and inclined to giggle and to herd together, squire and lady dressed almost similarly in tweed, and not differing much as to figure either, the sons very tall and slim, and slightly ashamed, the daughters rather taller and slimmer, in light muslins and large hats, all whispering together, half propitiatory, half on the defensive, and casting suspicious glances at everyone else. Amongst these groups Nutley discerned the young Brazilian, graceful as an antelope amongst cattle, and, going to the window, he saw the white Rolls-Royce silently manoeuvring amongst the gigs and the waggonettes.

'Regular bean-feast, ain't it?' said Stanforth's voice behind him. 'You ought to have had a merry-go-round and a gipsy booth, Nutley.' Nutley uncovered his teeth in a nervously polite smile. He looked at his watch, and decided that it was time the London motors began to arrive. Also the train was due. Most of those who came by train would have to walk from the station; it wasn't far across the village and down the avenue to the house.

He could see the advance guard already, walking in batches of two and three. And there was Farebrother; silly old Farebrother, with his rosy face, and his big spectacles, and his woolly white curls under the broad hat. Not long to wait now. The auctioneer's men were at their posts; most of the chairs in the gallery were occupied, only the front rows being left empty owing to diffidence; the auctioneer himself, Mr Webb, had arrived and stood talking to Colonel Stanforth, with an air of unconcern, on any topic other than the sale.

The farms and outlying portions were to be dealt with first, then the house and the contents of the house, then the park, and the building lots that had been carved out of the park and that were especially dear to Nutley. It would be a long sale, and probably an exciting one. He hoped there would be competition over the house. He knew that several agencies were after it, but thought that he would place his money on the Brazilian.

A continuous stir of movement and conversation filled the gallery. People came up to Nutley and asked him questions in whispers, and some of the big dealers nodded to him. Nearly all the men had their catalogues and pencils ready; some were reading the booklet. The Brazilian slipped into a prominent seat, accompanied by his solicitor. A quarter to twelve. The garden was deserted now, for everyone had crowded into the house. Five minutes to twelve. Mr Webb climbed up into his high chair, adjusted his glasses, and began turning over some papers on the desk before him.

A message was brought to Nutley: Mr Webb would be much obliged if he would remain at hand to answer any point that might be raised. Nutley was only too glad. He went and leant against the auctioneer's chair, at the back, and from there surveyed the whole length of the room. Rows of expectant people. People leaning against the walls and in the doorways. The gaitered farmers. The gentry. The dealers. The clerks and small fry. The men in green baize aprons. Such a crowd as the gallery had never seen.

'Lot one, gentlemen…'

The sharp rap of the auctioneer's little ivory hammer, and the buzz in the room was stilled; throats were cleared, heads raised.

'Lot one, gentlemen. Three cottages adjoining the station, with one acre of ground; coloured green on plan. What bids, gentlemen? Anyone start the bidding? Five hundred guineas? four hundred? Come, come, gentlemen, please,' admonishing them, 'we have a great deal to get through. I ask your kind co-operation.'

Knocked down at seven hundred and fifty guineas. Nutley noted the sum in the margin of his catalogue. Webb was a capital auctioneer: he bustled folk, he chaffed them, he got them into a good temper, he made them laugh so that their purses laughed wide in company. He had a jolly round face, a twinkling eye, and a rosebud in his buttonhole. Five hundred and fifty for the next lot, two cottages; so far, so good.

'Now, gentlemen, we come to something a little more interesting: the farmhouse and lands known as Orchards. An excellent house, and a particularly fine brew of ale kept there, too, as I happen to know – though that doesn't go with the house.' (The audience laughed; it appreciated that kind of pleasantry.) 'What offers, gentlemen? Two hundred acres of fine pasture and arable, ten acres of shaw, twenty acres of first-class fruit trees…' 'That's so, sir,' from Chase's old apple-dealer friend at the back of the room, and heads were turned smilingly towards him. 'There spoke the best authority in the county,' cried the auctioneer, catching on to this, 'as nice a little property as you could wish. I've a good mind to start the bidding myself. Fifty guineas – I'll put up fifty guineas. Who'll go one better?' The audience laughed again; Mr Webb had a great reputation as a wag. Nutley caught sight of Farebrother's full-moon face at the back of the room, perfunctorily smiling.

The tenant began bidding for his own farm; he had been to Nutley to see whether a mortgage could be arranged, and Nutley knew the extent of his finances. The voice of the auctioneer followed the bidding monotonously up, 'Two thousand guineas... two thousand two hundred... come, gentlemen, we're wasting time... two thousand five hundred...'

Knocked down to the farmer at three thousand five hundred guineas. A wink passed between Nutley and the purchaser: the place had not sold very well, but Nutley's firm would get a commission on the mortgage.

Lot four. Jakes' cottage. Nutley remembered that Chase had once commented on Jakes' garden, and he remembered also that old Miss Chase used to favour Jakes and his flowers: he supposed sarcastically that it was hereditary among the Chases to favour Jakes. That same stab of malice came back to him, and this time it included Jakes: the man made himself ridiculous over his garden, carrying (as he boasted) soil and leaf-mould home for it for miles upon his back; that was all over now, and his cottage would first be sold as a building site and then pulled down.

He caught sight of Jakes, standing near a window, his every-day corduroy trousers tied as usual with string round the knees; he looked terribly embarrassed, and was swallowing hard; the Adam's apple in his throat moved visibly above his collar. He stood twisting his cap between his hands. Nutley derisively watched him, saying to himself that the fellow might be on the point of making a speech. Surely he wasn't going to bid, a working man on perhaps forty shillings a week! Nutley was taken up and entertained by this idea, when a stir at the door distracted his attention; he glanced to see who the latecomer was, and perceived Chase.

15

Chase entered hurriedly, and asked a question of a man standing by; he looked haggard and ill, but the answer to his question appeared to reassure him, and he slipped quietly to the chair that somebody offered him. Several people recognised him, and pointed him out to one another. Nutley stared, incredulous and indignant. Just like his sly ways again! Why take the trouble to write and say he was detained by press of business, when he had every intention of coming? Sly. Well, might he enjoy himself, listening to the sale of his house; Nutley, with an angry shrug, wished him joy.

Meanwhile Mr Webb's voice, above him, continued to advocate Jakes' cottage, 'either as a building site or as a tearoom, gentlemen; I needn't point out to you the advantages of either in the heart of a picturesque village on a well-frequented motor route. The garden's only a quarter of an acre, but you have seen it today on your way from the station; a perfect picture. What offers? Come! We're disposed to let this lot go cheap as the cottage is in need of repair. It's a real chance for somebody.'

'One hundred guineas,' called out a fat man, known to Nutley as the proprietor of a hotel in Eastbourne.

'And fifty,' said Jakes in a trembling voice.

Nutley suppressed a cackle of laughter.

'And seventy-five,' said the fat man, after glaring at Jakes.

'Two hundred,' said Jakes.

Chase sat on the edge of his chair, twisting his fingers together and keeping his eyes fixed on Jakes. So the man was trying to save his garden! – and the flowers, through whose roots he said he would put a bagginhook sooner than let them pass to a stranger. Where did he imagine he could get the money, poor fool! The fat man was after the cottage for some commercial enterprise. What had the auctioneer suggested – a tearoom?

That was it, without a doubt – a tearoom! A painted signboard hanging out to attract motorists; little tin tables in the garden, perhaps, on summer evenings.

The fat man ran Jakes up to two hundred and fifty before Jakes began to falter. Something in the near region of two hundred and fifty was the limit, Chase guessed, to which his secret and inscrutable financial preparations would run. What plans had he made before coming, poor chap; what plans, full of a lamentable pathos, to meet the rivalry of those who might possibly have designs upon his tenement? Surely not very crafty plans, or very adequate? They had reached two hundred and seventy-five. Jakes was distressed; and to Nutley, scornfully watching, as to Chase, compassionately watching, and as to the auctioneer, impartially watching, it was clear that neither conscience nor prudence counselled him to go any further.

'Two hundred and seventy-five guineas are bid,' said the voice of the auctioneer; 'two hundred and seventy-five guineas,' – pause – 'going, going…'

'Three hundred,' brought out Jakes, upon whose forehead sweat was standing. 'And ten,' said the fat man remorselessly.

Jakes shook his head as the auctioneer looked at him in inquiry.

'Three hundred and ten guineas *are* bid,' said the auctioneer, 'three hundred and ten guineas,' his voice rising and trailing, 'no more? – a little more, sir, come!' in persuasion to Jakes, who shook his head again. 'Lot four, gentlemen, going for the sum of three hundred and ten guineas, going, going, gone.' The hammer came down with a sharp tap, and Mr Webb leant across his desk to take the name and address of the purchaser.

Jakes began making his way out of the room. He had the shameful air of one who has failed before all men in the single audacity of his lifetime. For him, lot four had been the lot that must rivet everyone's attention; it had been not an episode but the apex. Chase saw him slink out, burdened by disgrace. It would be several hours before he regained the spirit to put the bagginhook through the flowers.

'Lot five...' Callous as Roman sports proceeding on the retreat of the conquered gladiator. Scatter sand on the blood! Chase sat on, dumbly listening, the auctioneer's voice and the rap of the hammer twanging, metallic, across the chords of his bursting head. He had surely been mad to come – to expose himself to this pain, madder than poor Jakes, who at least came with a certain hope. What had brought him – his body felt curiously light; he knew only that he had slipped out of his lodgings at six that morning, had found his way into trains, his limbs performing the necessary actions for him, while his mind continued remote and fixed only upon the distant object towards which he was being rapidly carried. His house – during this miserable week in Wolverhampton, what had they been doing to his house? – perpetrating what infamy? Sitting in the train his mind glazed into that one concentration – Blackboys; he had wondered dimly whether he would indeed find the place where he had left it, among the trees, or whether he had dreamt it, under an enchantment; whether life in Wolverhampton – his office, his ledgers, his clerks, his lodgings – were not the only reality? Still his limbs, intelligent servants, had carried him over the difficulties of the cross-country journey, rendering him at the familiar station – a miracle. As he crossed the stile at the bend of the footpath – for he had taken the short cut across the fields from the station – he had come upon the house, he had heard his breath sob in his throat, and he had repressed the impulse to stretch out both his hands... With his eagerness his steps had quickened. It was the house, though not as he knew it. Not slumbrous. Not secluded. Carriages and motors under the trees, grooms and chauffeurs strolling about, idly staring. The house unveiled, prostituted; yes, it was like seeing one's mistress in a slave market. He had bounded up the steps into the hall, where a handful of loafing men had quizzed him impertinently. The garden door opposite stood open, and he could see right up the garden; was puzzled, in passing, because he missed the peacocks parading the blazon of their spread tails. The familiarity of the proportions closed instantly round him. Wolverhampton receded; *this* was reality; *this* was home.

He had gone up the staircase, his head reeling with anger when he saw that the pictures had been taken down from their places, and stood propped along the walls of the upper passage, ticketed and numbered. He had madly resented this interference with his property. Then he had gone into the gallery, sick and blind, dazzled by the sight that met him there, as though he had come suddenly into too strong a light. He had assured himself at once that they had not yet reached the selling of the house. Still his – and he stumbled into a chair and assisted at the demolition of Jakes.

The windows were wide open; bees blundered in and out; the tops of the woods appeared, huge green pillows; above them the cloudless sky; Midsummer day. Where, then, was the sweet harmony of the house and garden that waited upon the lazy hours of such a day? Driven out by dust and strangers, the Long Gallery made dingy by rows of chairs, robbed of its own mellow furnishing, robbed of its silence by sharp voices; the violation of sanctuary. Chase sat with his fingers knotted together between his knees. Perhaps a score of people in that room knew him by sight; to the others he was an onlooker; to the ones who knew him, an owner hoping for a good price. They must know he was poor – the park fence was lichen-covered and broken down in many places; the road up to the house was overgrown with weeds. Poor – obliged to sell; the place, for all its beauty, betrayed its poverty. Only the farmers looked prosperous. (Those farmers must have prospered better than they ever admitted, for here was one of them buying in at a most respectable figure the house and lands he rented.) His over-excited senses quietening down a little, he paid attention to the progress of the sale, finding there nothing but the same intolerable pain; the warmth of his secret memory stirred by the chill probe of the words he heard pronounced from the auctioneer's desk – 'ten acres of fallow, known as Ten-Acre Field, with five acres, three roods, and two perches of wood, including a quantity of fine standing timber to the value of two hundred and fifty pounds' – he knew that wood; it was free of undergrowth, and the bare tree trunks rose like columns straight out of a sea of bluebells: two hundred and fifty pounds' worth of standing timber. Walking in Ten-Acre Field outside the edge of that wood he had scared many a rabbit that vanished into the wood with a frisk of white tail, and had startled the rusty pheasants up into heavy flight.

Knocked down to the farmer who had just bought in his farm.

He didn't much resent the fields and woods going to the farmers. If anyone other than himself must have them, let it be the yeomen by whom they were worked and understood. But the house – there was the rub, the anguish. Nutley had mentioned a Brazilian (Nutley's most casual word about the house, or a buyer for the house, had remained indelibly stamped on Chase's mind). He looked about now, for the first time since he had come into the room, and discovered Nutley leaning against the auctioneer's high chair, then he discovered the young man who must certainly be the Brazilian in question, and all the dread which had been hitherto, so to speak, staved off, now smote him with its imminence as his eyes lighted on the unfamiliar, insouciant face.

The new owner, lounging there, insufferable, graceful, waiting without impatience, so insultingly unperturbed! Cool as a cucumber, that young man, accustomed to find life full of a persevering amiability. Chase made a movement to rise; he wanted to fly the room, to escape an ordeal that appalled his soul, but his shyness held him down: he could not create a sensation before so many people. Enraged as he was by the weakness that caught him thus, and prevented him from saving himself while there was still time, he yet submitted, pinned to his chair, enduring such misery as made all his previous grief sink to the level of mere discomfort. He yearned even after hours that lay in the past, and that at the time of their being had seemed to him, in all truth, sufficiently weighted; the hours he had spent standing beside the dealers during their minute examination of his possessions, while he wrung out his pitiable flippancies; then, in those days, he had known that ultimately they would take their leave, and that he would be left to turn back alone into his house, greeted by the dog beating his tail against the legs of the furniture, as pleased as his master; or the hour when, sitting in this very gallery (how different then!), he had read through Nutley's offensive booklet, and had not known whether it was chiefly anger or pain that drove extravagant ideas of revolt across his mind; those hours by comparison now appeared to him elysian – he had tasted then but the froth on the cup of bitterness of which he now reached the dregs.

God, how quickly they were getting through the lots! Lot fourteen was already reached, and sixteen was the house. Surely no soul could withstand such pressure, but must crumble like a crushed shell? When they actually reached lot sixteen, when he heard the auctioneer start off with his 'Now, gentlemen...' what would he do then, how would he behave? It was no longer shyness that held him, but fascination, and a physical sickness that made his body clammy and moist although he was shivering with cold. Fear must be like this, and from his heart he pitied all those who were mortally afraid. He noticed that several people were looking at him, amongst others Nutley, and he thought that he must be losing control of his reason, for it seemed to him that Nutley's face was yellow and pointed, and was grinning at him with a squinting malevolence, an oblique derision, altogether fantastic, and pushed up quite close to him, although in reality Nutley was some way off. He put up his hand to his forehead, and one or two people made an anxious movement towards him, as though they thought he was going to faint. He rejected them with a vague gesture, and at that moment heard the auctioneer say, 'Lot sixteen, gentlemen...'

16

There was a general stir in the room, of chairs being shifted, and legs uncrossed and recrossed. Mr Webb gave a little cough, while he laid aside his catalogue in favour of the more elaborate booklet, which he opened on the desk in front of him, flattening down the pages with a precise hand. He drew himself up, took off his glasses, and tapped the booklet with them, surveying his audience. 'As you know, ladies and gentlemen – as, in fact, this monograph, which you have all had in your hands, will have told you if you did not know it before – we have in Blackboys one of the most perfect examples of the Elizabethan manor house in England. I don't think I need take up your time and my own by enlarging upon that, or by pointing out the historical and artistic value of the property about to be disposed of; I can safely leave the ancient building, and the monograph so ably prepared by my friend Mr Nutley, to speak for themselves. It only remains for me to beg those intending to bid, to second my efforts in putting the sale through as quickly as possible, for we still have a large portion of the catalogue to deal with, and to bear in mind that a reserve figure of reasonable proportions has been placed upon the manor house and surrounding grounds. Lot sixteen, the manor house known as Blackboys, the pleasure grounds of eight acres, and one hundred and twenty-five acres of park land adjoining.'

A short silence succeeded Mr Webb's little speech. The Brazilian and his solicitor whispered together. The representatives of the various agencies looked at one another to see who would take the first step. Finally a voice said, 'Eight thousand guineas.'

'Come, come,' smiled Mr Webb.

'Nine thousand,' said another voice.

'I told you, gentlemen, that a reasonable reserve had been placed upon this lot,' said the auctioneer in a tone of restrained impatience, 'and you must all of you be sufficiently acquainted with the standard of sale-room prices to know that that nine thousand guineas comes nowhere near a reasonable figure for a property such as the one we have now under consideration.'

Thus rebuked, the man who had first spoken said, 'All right – twelve thousand.'

'And five hundred,' said the second man.

'Sticky, sticky,' murmured Nutley, shaking his head.

Still neither the Brazilian nor his solicitor made any sign. The agents were evidently unwilling to show their hands; then a little man began to bid on behalf of an American standing at his elbow: 'Thirteen thousand guineas.'

This stirred the agents, and between them all the bidding crackled up to eighteen thousand. Mr Webb, judging that the American was probably good for twenty or twenty-five, and wishing to entice the Brazilian into competition, said in the same resigned tone, 'I am unwilling to withdraw this lot, but I am afraid we cannot afford to waste time in this fashion.'

'Make it twenty, sir,' called out the American, 'and let's get a move on.'

'Thank you, sir,' said Mr Webb, in the midst of a laugh. 'I am bid twenty thousand guineas for lot sixteen, twenty thousand guineas are bid... and five hundred on my right... twenty-one thousand on my left... thank you again, sir: twenty-two thousand guineas. Twenty-two thousand guineas. Surely no one wishes to see this lot withdrawn? Twenty-two thousand guineas. And five hundred. And two hundred and fifty more. Twenty-two thousand seven hundred and fifty guineas...'

'Twenty-three thousand,' said the solicitor who had come with the Brazilian.

People craned forward now to see and to hear. The Brazilian had been generally pointed out as the most likely buyer, and until he or his man took up the bidding it could be disregarded as preliminary. The small fry of the agents served to run it up into workable figures, after which it would certainly pass beyond them. The duel, it was guessed, would lie between the American and the Brazilian.

'Twenty-four thousand,' called out one of the agents in a sort of dying flourish.

'And five hundred,' said another, not to be outdone.

'Twenty-five thousand,' said the Brazilian's solicitor.

'Twenty-five thousand guineas are bid,' said the auctioneer. 'Twenty-five thousand guineas. I am authorised by Mr Nutley, the solicitor acting for this estate, to tell you...' he glanced down at Nutley, who nodded, '... to tell you that this sum had already been offered, and refused, at the estate office. If, therefore, no gentleman is willing to pass beyond twenty-five thousand guineas, I shall be compelled... and five hundred, thank you, sir. Twenty-five thousand five hundred guineas.'

Most people present supposed that this sum came very near to being adequate, and a murmur to this effect passed up and down the room. People looked at Chase, who was as white as death and sat with his eye fixed upon the floor. The American, good-humouredly enough, was trying to take the measure of the unruffled young man; judging from the slight shrug he gave, he did not think he stood much chance, but nevertheless he called, 'Keep the ball rolling. Two hundred and fifty more.'

The room began to take sides, most preferring the straightforward vulgarity of the jolly American to the outlandishness of the young man, which baffled and put them ill at their ease. (Nutley found time to think that the youth of the neighbourhood would need some time before it recovered from the influence of that young man, even if he were to pass away with the day.) Those who had the habit of sale rooms thought Chase lucky in having two men, both keen, against one another to run up a high price. They bent forward with their elbows on their knees and their chins in their hands, to listen.

'And two hundred and fifty more,' capped the solicitor.

'Twenty-six thousand guineas are bid,' said Mr Webb, who by now was leaning well over his desk and whose glances kept travelling sharply between the rivals. He was sure that the Brazilian intended, if necessary, to go to thirty thousand.

'Twenty-seven,' said the American, recklessly.

'Twenty-eight,' said the solicitor after a word with his employer.

The American shook his head; he was very jovial and friendly, and bore no malice. He laughed, but he shook his head.

'If that is your last word, gentlemen, I regret to say that the lot must be withdrawn, as the reserve has not been reached,' said Mr Webb. 'I am sure that Mr Nutley will pardon me the slight irregularity in giving you this information, under the exceptional circumstances...' Nutley assented; he greatly enjoyed being referred to, especially now in Chase's presence... 'I only do so in order to give you the chance of continuing should you wish...'

'All right, anything to make a running,' said the American, who was certainly the favourite of the excited and eager audience; 'two hundred and fifty better than the last bid.'

The auctioneer caught the Brazilian's nod.

'I am bid twenty-eight thousand five hundred guineas... twenty-nine thousand,' he added, as the American nodded to him.

'Thirty,' said the Brazilian quietly.

He had not spoken before, and every gaze was turned upon him as, perfectly cool, he stood leaning against the wall in the bay of a window. He was undisturbed, from the sleekness of his head down to his immaculate shoes. He had all the assurance of one who is certain of having spoken the last word.

'I'm out of this,' said the American.

'Thirty thousand guineas *are* bid,' said the auctioneer; 'for lot sixteen thirty thousand guineas. THIRTY THOUSAND GUINEAS,' he enunciated; 'going, for the sum of thirty thousand guineas, going, going...'

Chase tottered to his feet.

'Thirty-one thousand,' he cried in a strangled voice, 'thirty-one thousand!'

17

Of all the astonished people in that room, perhaps not the least astonished was the auctioneer. He had never seen Chase before, and naturally thought that he had to deal with an entirely new candidate. He adjusted his glasses to stare at the solitary figure upright among the rows of seated people, standing with a trembling hand still outstretched. He had just time to notice with concern that Chase was deathly pale, his face carved and hollowed, before habit reasserted itself, and he checked the 'gone!' that had almost left his lips, to resume his chronicle of the bidding with 'Thirty-one thousand guineas... any advance on thirty-one thousand guineas?' and cocked his eye at the Brazilian.

The Brazilian, equally surprised, had never before seen Chase either. What was this fierce little man, who had shot up out of the ground so turbulently to dispute his prize? He had not supposed that it would be necessary to go beyond the thirty thousand; nevertheless he was prepared to do so, and to make his determination clear he continued with the bidding himself instead of leaving it to his solicitor. 'And five hundred,' he said.

'Thirty-five thousand,' said Chase.

The sensation he would have created by escaping from the room half an hour earlier was nothing to the sensation he was creating now. But he was exalted far beyond shyness or false shame. He never noticed the excited flutter all over the room, or the extraordinary agitation of Nutley, who was saying 'He's mad! He's mad!' while frantically trying to attract the auctioneer's attention. Chase was oblivious to all this. He stood, feeling himself inspired by some divine breath, the room a blur before him, and a current of power, quite indomitable, surging through his veins. Infatuation. Genius. They must be like this. This certainty. This unmistakable purpose. This sudden clearing away of all irrelevant preoccupations. Vistas opened down into all the obscurities that had always shadowed and confused his brain: the secret was to find oneself, to know what one really wanted, what one really cared for, and to go for it straight. Wolverhampton? Moonshine! He was no longer pale, nor did he keep his eyes shamefully bent upon the ground; he was flushed, embattled; his nostrils dilated and working.

But everyone else thought him crazy, people sober watching the vaingloriousness of a man drunk. Even the auctioneer allowed an expression of surprise to cross his face, and varied his formula by saying suavely, 'Did I understand you to say thirty-five thousand, sir? Thirty-five thousand guineas are bid.'

Drunk. As a man drunk. Everything appeared smothered to his senses; intense, yet remote. His head light and swimming. Everything at a great distance. The crowd around him, stirring, murmurous, but meaningless. The auctioneer, perched up there, a diminutive figure, miles away. Voices, muffled but enormously significant, conveying threats, conveying combat. All leagued against him. This was battle; all the faces were hostile. Or so he imagined. He was glad of it. Fighting for his house? No, no! More, far more than that: fighting for the thing he loved. Fighting to shield from rape the thing he loved. Fighting alone; come to his senses in the very nick of time. Even at this moment, when he needed every wit he had ever had at his command, he found time for a deep inward thankfulness that the illumination had not come too late or altogether passed him by. In the nick of time it had come, and he had recognised it; recognised it for what it was, and seized hold of it, and now, triumphantly, drunkenly, was holding his own in the face of all this dismay and opposition. Moreover, they could not defeat him. Bidding in these outrageous sums that need never be paid over, he was possessed of an inexhaustible fortune. Undefeatable – what confidence that gave him! The more hands turned against him the better. He challenged everybody; he hardly knew what he was saying, only that he leapt up in thousands, and that in spite of their astonishment and fury they were powerless against him: there was nothing criminal or even illegal in his buying in his own house if he wanted to.

And then the end, that came before he knew that it was imminent; the collapse of the Brazilian, whose expression had at last changed from deliberate indifference to real bad temper; the voice of the auctioneer, suavely asking for his name and his address; and his own voice, giving his name as though for the first time in his life he were not ashamed of it. And then Nutley, struggling across the room to him, snarling and yapping at him like a little enraged cur, quite vague and deprived of significance, but withal noisy, tiresome, and briefly perplexing; a Nutley disproportionately enraged, furiously gesticulating, spluttering at him, 'Are you going to play this damned fool game with the rest of the sale?' and his answer – he supposed he had given an answer, because of the announcement from the auctioneer's desk, which hushed the noisy room into sudden silence, 'I have to inform you, gentlemen, that lot sixteen, and the succeeding lots, which include the contents of the mansion, also the surrounding park, have been bought in, and that the sale is therefore at an end.'

And, in the midst of his bewilderment, the sensation of having his hand sought for and wrung, while he gazed down into Mr Farebrother's old rosy face and heard him say, half inarticulate with emotion, 'I'm so glad, Mr Chase, I congratulate you, I'm so glad, I'm so *glad.*'

18

Finally, the blessed peace and solitude, when the last stranger with the curious stare that was now common to them all had quitted the house, and the last motor had rolled away. Chase, leaning against a column of the porch, thought that thus must married lovers feel when after the confusion of their wedding they are at length left alone together. Certainly – with a wry twist to his lip – the events of the sale had tried him as sorely as any wedding. But here he was, having won, in possession, having driven away all that rabble; here he was in the warmth, and in the hush that sank back upon everything after the ceasing of all that hubbub; here he was left alone upon the field after that reckless victory. Poor? Yes, but he could work, he would manage; his poverty would not be bitter, it would be sweet. He suddenly stretched out his hands, and passion-ately laid them, palms flattened, against the bricks; bricks warm as their own rosiness with the sun they had drunk since morning.

Midsummer day. Swallows skimming after the insects above the moat. Their level wings almost grazed the water as they swooped. Midsummer day. All the mellowness of Blackboys, all the blood of the Chases, to culminate in this midsummer day. A marvellous summer. A persistently marvellous summer. He remembered the procession of days, the dawns and the dusks and the moon-bathed nights, that had hallowed his romance. He was inclined to believe that neither hatred nor its ugly kin could any longer find any place in his heart, which had been so uplifted and had seen so radiantly the flare of so many beacons lighting up the fields of wisdom. To cast off the slavery of the Wolverhamptons of this world. To know what one really wanted, what one really cared for, and to go for it straight. Wasn't that a good enough and simple enough working wisdom for a man to have attained? Simple enough, when it did nobody any harm – yet so few seemed to learn it.

Blackboys! Wolverhampton! What was Wolverhampton beside Blackboys? What was the promise of that mediocre ease beside the certainty of these exquisite privations? What was that drudgery beside this beauty, this pride, this quixotism?

Thane gambolled out, fawning and leaping round Chase, as Fortune opened the door of the house.

'Will you be having dinner, sir,' he asked demurely, 'in the dining room or in the garden this evening?'

Biographical note

Victoria Mary Sackville-West, known throughout her life as Vita, was born to Lionel Edward, 3rd Baron of Sackville, and his first cousin Victoria Sackville-West, at Knole House in Kent on the 9th of March 1892. As the setting of her early life, Knole had a profound effect on Sackville-West, inspiring a lifelong passion for gardening for which she was recognised by the Royal Horticultural Society in 1955.

Sackville-West began writing as a child and published her first work, the verse drama *Chatterton*, in 1909, aged seventeen. By this time she had already met Violet Keppel, later Trefusis, with whom she was to have an affair which would endure until long after both women were married. The pair eloped to the Continent several times, having to be coaxed back to England by their husbands. The affair inspired Sackville-West's second novel, *Challenge*, written in 1923. Perhaps the most notorious episode of Sackville-West's life was her later affair with Virginia Woolf, to whom she was introduced by the art critic Clive Bell in 1922. Sackville-West famously inspired Woolf's *Orlando*.

Although her lesbian liaisons achieved a certain notoriety, Sackville-West was married in 1913, aged twenty-one, to Harold Nicolson, also a bisexual with whom she had a famously open relationship. The pair remained married until Sackville-West's death and had two sons, Nigel and Benedict. Nicolson was supportive of Sackville-West's horticultural passions, and in 1929 the family acquired and moved to Sissinghurst Castle in Kent, then virtually derelict. The property, now owned by the National Trust, owes its current splendour to Sackville-West. Horticultural pursuits also inspired her long narrative poem, *The Land*, for which she was awarded the Hawthornden Prize in 1926, and from 1946 she wrote a gardening column for *The Observer*.

Sackville-West's best-known writings, *The Edwardians* and *All Passion Spent*, were written in the early 1930s, and she won the Hawthornden Prize a second time in 1933 for her *Collected Poems*. She was made a Companion of Honour for literature in 1946, and died of cancer in June 1962.

HESPERUS PRESS

Hesperus Press, as suggested by the Latin motto, is committed to bringing near what is far – far both in space and time. Works written by the greatest authors, and unjustly neglected or simply little known in the English-speaking world, are made accessible through new translations and a completely fresh editorial approach. Through these classic works, the reader is introduced to the greatest writers from all times and all cultures.

For more information on Hesperus Press, please visit our website:
www.hesperuspress.com

ET REMOTISSIMA PROPE

MODERN VOICES